"I want to help catch this guy before he strikes again. What if he's planning his next attack now? What if I'm not so lucky the next time? What if he hurts Gus? Or another woman? The more input I can give the police, the faster this lunatic can be caught, and the sooner I can sleep again. Preferably before Christmas."

Cade moved his hands to his hips. He couldn't hold her captive or tell her what to do, but he could stick close, and he could keep her safe. "All right," he conceded, "but you have to stay in my sight at all times, preferably in reach, and if I say it's time to go, we need to leave immediately."

Lyndy nodded. "Agreed," she said. "And I think we should pretend to be a couple." She raised a palm. "Hear me out."

Cade worked to control his stunned expression. He'd endured some wild requests from clients before, but those usually involved him staying out of the way, not faking a romantic relationship.

MARINE
PROTECTOR

———

Julie Anne Lindsey

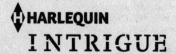

HARLEQUIN
INTRIGUE

To Lyndy.

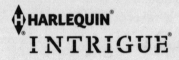

INTRIGUE®

ISBN-13: 978-1-335-13678-7

Marine Protector

Copyright © 2020 by Julie Anne Lindsey

Recycling programs
for this product may
not exist in your area.

This edition published by arrangement with Harlequin Books S.A.

For questions and comments about the quality of this book, please contact us at CustomerService@Harlequin.com.

Harlequin Enterprises ULC
22 Adelaide St. West, 40th Floor
Toronto, Ontario M5H 4E3, Canada
www.Harlequin.com

Printed in U.S.A.

Julie Anne Lindsey is an obsessive reader who was once torn between the love of her two favorite genres: toe-curling romance and chew-your-nails suspense. Now she gets to write both for Harlequin Intrigue. When she's not creating new worlds, Julie can be found carpooling her three kids around northeastern Ohio and plotting with her shamelessly enabling friends. Winner of the Daphne du Maurier Award for Excellence in Mystery/Suspense, Julie is a member of International Thriller Writers, Romance Writers of America and Sisters in Crime. Learn more about Julie and her books at julieannelindsey.com.

Books by Julie Anne Lindsey

Harlequin Intrigue

Fortress Defense

Deadly Cover-Up
Missing in the Mountains
Marine Protector

Garrett Valor

Shadow Point Deputy
Marked by the Marshal

Protectors of Cade County

Federal Agent Under Fire
The Sheriff's Secret

Visit the Author Profile page at Harlequin.com.

CAST OF CHARACTERS

Lyndy Wells—Single mother of an infant son, caught in the sights of a serial killer.

Cade Lance—Former marine and cofounder of Fortress Defense, assigned to protect Lyndy and her son from a determined serial killer.

Gus Wells—Five-month-old son of Lyndy.

Sawyer Lance—Cade's older brother, former army ranger and founding member of Fortress Defense.

Jack Hale—Fortress Defense team member partnering with Cade to protect Lyndy and her son.

The Kentucky Tom Cat Killer—Serial rapist and murderer circling small Kentucky communities, determined to make Lyndy Wells his next victim.

Detective Owens—Local detective assigned to Lyndy's case after the initial attack.

Special Agent Maxwell—Federal agent leading the charge to identify and capture the Kentucky Tom Cat Killer.

Chapter One

Rivulets of sweat ran down Lyndy Wells's temples and between her shoulder blades as she trekked back in the direction of her car, having completed another hefty evening walk. Toting thirty extra pounds was enough to make anyone sweat, but coupled with the uncomfortable weight of winter boots and her wool maternity coat, the act was exhausting. Not only did she have fifteen pounds of baby weight left to lose, she had the baby himself strapped to her chest in a snowsuit and carrier she'd initially suspected might require three engineers and a rocket scientist just to put on.

Gus was already five months old, and the pressure was on to lose those unwanted pounds. It was late in the season, and before long, the snow would come to her northern Kentucky town. Then her evening walks would go from tolerably chilly to downright impossible. Until then, she'd keep doing her best to take eight thousand steps a day, or as many as possible while carrying her son. At the moment she just wanted to get to her car, collapse behind the wheel and gulp the spare bottle of water she kept in the console.

She paused near the lake to bend and lift each rubbery leg, hoping to alleviate the growing burn in her hamstrings and catch her breath. A smattering of dried leaves skated across the still water where ducks and moms with bread-bag-wielding toddlers had gathered regularly on summer evenings. The ducks still made an appearance, but the families rarely did. The days were too short now, and Lyndy imagined most folks had fallen into a new evening routine. Unlike her. Gus was sound asleep against her chest now, as he normally was by this portion of the workout, but he was sure to be wide-awake when they got home. Just in time to make it impossible for her to shower right away.

The sun was low on the horizon as Lyndy settled into a slower, cool-down pace, the apricot and amber sky quickly giving way to twilight. Unfortunately, the same mountain shade she'd savored in the late summer afternoons resembled an ominous cover by dinnertime these days. She frequently imagined coyotes or bobcats creeping out from behind her car as she strapped Gus into his rear-facing car seat with complicated five-point safety harness. Another baby item probably designed by NASA.

She rubbed Gus's back as she pushed on, only to stop a few steps further when the tiny hairs along her neck rose with the breeze. Her intuition spiked a silent warning, but there was nothing and no one in sight to be wary of. She picked up her pace anyway, filled with renewed motivation to reach the safety of her car. The strange, nearly indescribable sensation plucked her already tightened skin, insisting something was simply *wrong,* and her gut pinched and flipped with every step.

She crossed the little wooden bridge from the park's walking path to the parking lot at a clip, already unearthing her keys and beeping the doors unlocked. Her headlights flashed on in response, adding a mixture of light and new shadows to her world.

"Almost there," she whispered, as much an encouragement to Gus as to herself. "A few more steps and we'll be locked in tight." The muscles along her neck and shoulders bunched, and her heart climbed as she came within steps of the car.

The wind blew again, and a strange scent caught Lyndy's nose. Not floral. Not natural. She couldn't name it. Couldn't place it, and it only alarmed her further. Not cologne. Not perfume. She broke into a jog, fear running its icy fingers along her spine and into her sweaty hair.

Her heavy breaths and footfalls stirred the baby on her chest. "Shh," she cooed. "Shh. Shh. Shh. It's okay. Mama's got you."

Finally, Lyndy wrapped panicked and trembling fingers around the handle of her car door, and for one brief heartbeat, they were safe.

Then her head jerked back with the force of a bull. Long, angry fingers clamped over her mouth and curled deep into the hair at the base of her neck. A scream locked in her throat, strangled silent by terror. The car keys clattered at her feet.

Confusion crushed every thought in Lyndy's head. Her fight-or-flight response was set to *flight*, and she cradled her baby with both arms, attempting to change their backward momentum and break free.

Gus struggled in his coat and carrier, a tiny whimper of complaint breaking free.

Lyndy dug her heels into the ground, but the hand only yanked her back again, harder, dragging her away from the lot. Her feet twisted and faltered beneath her. She flailed one arm for balance, while the other attempted to hold Gus tight.

The soul-crushing realization that this was how she would die, alone in a park where children fed ducks and moms pushed strollers, forced the confusion from her mind. She knew with pinpoint clarity that her son would be orphaned, become a foster child, a ward of the state, *if he was spared.*

If she didn't fight.

Adrenaline ignited in her veins like electricity on a power-plant fence.

This would *not* be her end, and it damn sure wouldn't be her son's. She let herself go limp, dropping the full weight of her new, heavier body onto the ground.

Lyndy was no longer tired. She was no longer

weak or fat or out of shape, or any of the other things she'd cursed herself for on the nightly two-mile walk. She was a mother bear with a cub to defend, and she'd do it or die trying.

Her assailant stumbled beneath the sudden change, and when he loosened his grip on her head to clutch her beneath the arms, Lyndy began to fight. He lifted her off the ground with some effort, pressing her back to his chest once more, this time tightening one forearm across her throat.

She slammed her boot against his shin, then his knee, then his instep. She aimed the point of her bent elbow into the meat below his ribs, and when his grip loosened again, Lyndy screamed. She gave another hearty thrust of her foot, and a flurry of curses flew from the assailant's lips.

Lyndy bounded forward, holding tight to her screaming baby and sliding over the wet grass along the lake's edge. A feral growl erupted behind her, but she wouldn't look back. She couldn't process, couldn't think. Her body had switched its goal from flight to fight, and back again. Now all she could do was run. She fumbled up the little grassy hill, sliding in goose mess and turning her ankles over rocks and sticks. Down to her knees, then up again, away from the danger, away from death, into the street beyond the parking lot where she'd dropped her keys.

Gus's cries rang in her ears. She had to get him as far away from the man as possible.

The sudden blinding force of headlights trapped

her in their glow, and Lyndy threw up her arms to protect her baby from an impact that didn't come.

Instead, the vehicle stopped. Two front doors cracked open and dark figures climbed out. "Ma'am?" the slow, steady drawl of an unknown man asked, his figure manifesting gradually through bright headlight beams. A savior? Or another assailant? "Are you hurt?" He drew closer, and Lyndy stepped back. The man lifted his palms, and Lyndy recognized the familiar navy blue uniform of an EMT.

A woman in matching gear appeared opposite him in the light. "Are you okay, ma'am?"

"No," Lyndy cried, overcome by the rush of assurance, safety and salvation, even as her baby screamed in hysterics. "We're not all right." Hot tears poured over her stinging cheeks as her knees buckled and her limbs began to shake.

THE HOSPITAL WAS bright and loud. Everything smelled of bleach, burnt coffee and bandages. People rushed in every direction, not appearing to see anything but what was directly before them. Maybe that was how they survived a career submerged in horrific and abounding tragedies.

Lyndy paced the overpolished floor beside the bed where her baby was poked and prodded by a nurse, doctor and what seemed like a half-dozen medical trainees. She'd been given a cursory evaluation and released from further care, allowed to oversee what was happening to Gus. Lyndy had a few scrapes and bruises on her knees and shins from falling, some light bruising across her mouth and neck from being manhandled, but nothing serious. Nothing lasting. It was Gus she was worried about. What if he had brain damage or shaken baby syndrome from all the jostling and jolting? What if she'd broken his tiny fingers, hands or arms during one of her falls, or damaged his hearing with her screams?

It was lucky she hadn't escaped a madman only to get her baby mowed down by a giant truck when she ran stupidly into the street outside the park.

Ambulance, she reminded herself. The vehicle had been an ambulance, and it had probably saved both their lives.

"Mrs. Wells?" A middle-aged man with a lab coat and stethoscope approached, hand extended.

Lyndy wrapped her arms more tightly around her middle. "Ms.," she corrected. She wasn't married. She thought everyone in their little community knew that by now. Half had probably attended Sam's funeral, or maybe it had only seemed that way. "How is he?" she asked, forcing the tougher thoughts away.

The man cleared his throat and dropped his hand back to his side. "I'm Dr. Mustav, and your little man is going to be just fine. I've given him a very thorough evaluation, and he appears to be completely unscathed. Thanks, no doubt, to his mother's quick thinking. Whatever you did out there, you saved his life. Both of your lives, really. I'm sure you're eager to get home, so I'll leave you to it." He raised his hand again slightly before letting it drop once more, and exited with a small nod.

Lyndy blinked back the tears. Gus was fine. *He was fine.* A deep rush of breath coursed through her, strong enough to knock her off balance.

"Ma'am?" A smiling nurse in teddy bear scrubs bopped cheerfully into view. "Gus is fast asleep now, but he's good to go whenever you're ready. I just need you to read over these discharge papers and sign before you leave." She handed Lyndy a clipboard with a stack of white pages and a pen. "Take as long as you need."

Lyndy dropped the clipboard onto the table and went to stroke her son's soft brown hair. His round cheeks were pink with color and his little button mouth worked in tiny circles, probably enjoying an imaginary bottle. A tear fell onto his forehead and he winced. Lyndy dried her eyes and his head quickly, then stroked his back gently until his mouth began to work on the bottle once more.

Suddenly, the weight of the night settled over her and pressed heavily on her soul. She backed into the uncomfortable bedside recliner, pulled her knees to her chest, wrapped her trembling arms around them and sobbed as quietly as possible against the dirty fabric of her pant legs.

She woke to the sound of her name. Her sore and tired eyes peeled open with considerable effort. Her feet had returned to the floor and her arms hung east and west across the arms of the chair.

"Ms. Wells?" An older gentleman in a suit and trench coat stood before her. His white hair and round glasses made him look like he belonged behind a library table or in a boardroom. The detective's shield on his coat said otherwise. "I'm Detective Harry Owens. How are you feeling?"

Her gaze jumped to the sleeping baby in the crib at her side. His chest rose and fell with strong, steady breaths.

"Okay," she said on instinct. "Better," she corrected.

"Good." He handed her a business card. "I've been assigned to your case, and I'd like to talk to you sometime. Are you feeling up to it?"

"No," she blurted. In fact, she doubted she'd ever feel up to reliving the horrors of her night. "Gus and I are free to go," she said, recalling the doctor and nurse's promise, "and it's been a terrible night, so we're going to go." The stack of papers caught her eye. She couldn't take Gus without at least signing the release papers. Could she? What would they do? Chase her down?

A noose tightened on her throat as the memory of being chased returned like a battering ram. She touched careful fingers to the tender skin where she could still feel the man's arm pressing down on her windpipe. Her cheeks flushed hot, and she concentrated on not passing out. Maybe she could stay long enough to sign the papers. Something else came to mind. "My car," she said. If she did run, where would she go? To a bus stop? Not without any money. She'd locked her purse in her glove box. "The ambulance brought us here."

"I can take you to your car," Detective Owens suggested. "We can talk on the way, or I can drive you home, if you'd prefer. You can give me your keys, and I'll bring the car to you later."

Her teeth began to chatter. "I dropped my keys in the lot.".

"Look, Ms. Wells," Detective Owens began, dragging another chair next to hers. He sat forward, resting his elbows on his knees, and he looked at her as if he truly cared. "I'm going to be honest with you about something that I don't think you're ready to hear right now, but truthfully, I don't know when a great time to tell you would be. So here it is. You fit the profile that federal officials have associated with a serial killer circling our community. Police departments in three neighboring counties are working with the FBI on similar cases, and they think your attack tonight is one that needs looking into. Unfortunately, they can't be sure, so I can't offer you much in the way of police protection other than some additional patrols of your street." He shifted his feet beneath the chair and locked his ankles, then folded his hands on his lap. "If you asked me for my advice, or if you were my daughter, I'd suggest you buy a gun and get to the range, but you don't look like my daughter, and you didn't ask for my advice, so I'll tell you this instead. There's a private protection firm in Lexington made up of former military men, good ones, honorable and smart ones. You could hire one of them to look after you until this thing gets sorted out, if you're interested. I understand their fees are fair, and they've been known to work pro bono where the need requires it. I'd say this situation fits the bill. They can probably get someone out here tonight. I've heard nothing but good things about them, and I don't make recommendations lightly. Ms. Wells? Can you hear me?"

Lyndy tried to nod her head, but it didn't move. "Serial killer?" she choked the words through a suddenly dry mouth, the syllables falling like stones from a sticky, swollen tongue.

Detective Owens didn't answer. He pulled a cell phone from the inside pocket of his coat and dialed before pressing it to his cheek.

She felt her attacker's hands on her. Felt his breath on her skin. The heat of him against her back. *A serial killer?* Bile rose in her throat, and her grip on the chair arms turned white.

"Ms. Wells?" The detective was on his feet. His phone was gone, and his coat was buttoned. "Come on, now." He outstretched a hand. "My wife's on her way. I think you might feel better with a woman along for the ride tonight. She's an angel, my Gracie. While we wait for her, you can finish those papers and we'll take you to get your car."

LYNDY PULLED INTO her driveway an hour later, and Detective Owens walked her inside. Her keys had been under her car, kicked slightly behind her wheel, her car still unlocked. Detective Owens made a loop through her home and waited on the porch before leaving while she locked up again. He'd assured her a member of the Fortress Defense team he'd told her about was on the way. Cade Lance, a former marine and honorably discharged vet. She triple-checked the locks and put on some coffee, then sat on the couch, watching through the front window for signs of trouble or her hired protector. She didn't even know what it cost to have a bodyguard, only that she couldn't afford not to have him, and Mr. Owens had set it all up while she'd been emotionally catatonic. Hopefully he'd been right about the sliding pay scale.

A flash of headlights opened her eyes. She hadn't realized that she'd closed them. A silhouette climbed down from the driver's side of a very tall, very black pickup truck outside her front window. A flutter of concern rocked through her as doubt over his identity crossed her mind: she hoped this was the man from Fortress Defense and not the man from the park. How did Detective Owens say he knew these guys? Were they buddies of his? All retired military? The beast of a truck looked nothing like Detective Owens's sensible sedan, and the lean silhouette moving forward with strong, confident swagger certainly didn't resemble the stout father figure who'd watched over her and Gus tonight.

The man took another step, and the motion sensor for her porch light switched on.

"Whoa," she whispered, rising to her knees on the couch for a better look through her front window. She drank in the broad shoulders and narrow hips of the unexpected cowboy with sincere appreciation. A large black Stetson cast long shadows over eyes that sent a chill skittering down her spine. Not a turn-and-run chill like the others she'd had tonight. This was the kind of tingle that made her insides flush hot, especially after she caught a glimpse of his square jaw and tight blue jeans.

The cowboy walked the length of her porch in both directions before returning to her front door and knocking.

Lyndy approached the door on unsteady legs and peeked through the small window before grabbing the knob.

His cool blue eyes met hers instantly, pale and fathomless in the thin porch light. "Ms. Wells. I'm Cade Lance, Fortress Defense. Detective Harry Owens called me."

Lyndy turned the knob, enjoying the veil of heat sliding across her skin at the sound of his slow Southern drawl, and then opened the door to meet her new personal protector.

Chapter Two

Cade waited outside the open door for the little blonde to look less shell-shocked before stepping inside. "I'm sorry if you've been waiting long. I know it's been an awful night. I got here as quickly as I could."

She scanned him with wide blue eyes, her lightly freckled cheeks flushing with color. "Come in." She locked the door behind him and tugged it twice before seeming to accept it as secure. "I'm Lyndy Wells. Thank you for coming on such short notice."

Cade offered her a hand to shake. "Cade Lance. Short notice comes with the job. I don't mind."

Her small, soft hand fitted easily into his larger, rougher one, and he felt the tremor she'd been hiding. This woman put up a good front, but she was terrified.

"Coffee?" she asked.

"All right." Cade nodded, and Lyndy hurried away. Her short blond hair didn't quite reach her narrow shoulders, and the cotton T-shirt and pants she wore seemed oddly large on her petite frame.

Cade followed her through the tidy house splattered in baby gear, blankets and toys. "Where should I put this?" he asked, swinging the black duffel bag off his shoulder. He had more in the truck, but the rest could wait for morning. The go-bag he kept at the ready had everything he'd need for now.

"Oh." She stopped abruptly and changed directions, heading down a long narrow hall. "Here." She swung the first door open and motioned him inside. Her cheeks darkened again as she approached the tall bed with at least fifty pillows in every shape and size. "I forgot to make it up. That bedding's probably been on there since I moved in last year. No one's ever needed the guest room."

Cade dropped his bag on the bed and gave the place a slow look. "This is just fine."

Stacks of boxes lined one wall, four high and two rows deep, as if she still needed to unpack. Most of them had the letters SAM scribbled across one side. The rest of the room looked as if his grandmother had decorated it. Pink-and-white floral everything, complete with a big round shag carpet beneath a pillow-filled rocking chair. The whole place smelled like vanilla. It was a far cry from his utilitarian apartment, and even farther from his living quarters overseas.

Lyndy headed back down the hall to the kitchen, and Cade followed again. He gave the rattle on the highchair beside the table a gentle shake. "Detective Owens said you have a baby?" She certainly didn't look like someone who'd recently had a baby. She barely looked old enough to own a home, but she was twenty-seven, according to the social media profiles he'd checked while packing for the assignment.

He was twenty-seven. Did he look like a kid to other people?

"I have a five-month-old son, Gus. Do you take cream or sugar?" she asked, offering him a cup of coffee.

"No. Thank you." He accepted the cup and gave the homey country kitchen a cursory look. Too many windows. French doors. Too many points of entry. "You live alone with your son?" he asked. It was a large home for one woman and a baby. At least three thousand square feet. A sprawling one-floor ranch.

"Yes," she answered softly.

Cade moved to the glass doors overlooking the rear patio and dark expanse of land. "How many acres are here?"

"Eight acres," she said. "We don't own as much as it seems. There just aren't any neighbors for a good quarter mile or more."

Cade turned back to her. "We? You and your boy?"

Lyndy frowned. "Yes."

Cade stepped in her direction, attempting to gauge her strange response. *Was there an ex-boyfriend? Ex-husband?*

She sighed. "I bought the property with my former fiancé early last year, and we moved in a couple weeks before the wedding was scheduled."

Cade folded his arms, balancing his steaming mug just below his lips. There was heartbreak in her eyes. The agonizing, life-altering kind. He'd seen it before. Lived through it himself. *Grief.* "I'm sorry about your loss."

Her shining blue eyes snapped in his direction, full of unshed tears. "How did you…" She let the question hang. "Thank you." She wet her lips and took a seat at the table. "He was on his way home from a weekend of fishing with friends. A long-haul trucker fell asleep at the wheel, crossed into oncoming traffic. That was that."

Cade adjusted his hat, unsure what to say from there. He tightened his stance and gave her time to continue or change the subject if she wanted. Surprisingly, he hoped she'd continue. There was something about her that made him curious in a number of ways, most of them unprofessional, but all of them genuine.

"Sam was older," she said. "Thirty-six. Some folks thought the age difference was weird, but it wasn't to us. He was a good man." She took her time sipping the coffee she'd poured for herself. "I guess you've lost plenty of good men, too. I hear you're just home from overseas."

"I am."

Lyndy ran a fingertip along the rim of her steaming mug. "Detective Owens said you were a marine."

"That's right." Cade shifted, uncomfortable with the questions directed at him. A wry smile caught his lips. Hadn't he done the same to her? It was necessary, he supposed, to get to know one another if he was going to live there temporarily and protect her. They needed a level of comfort and trust. "I was enlisted eight years. I did three tours overseas."

She tipped her head over one shoulder, maybe evaluating the answer. "Do you miss it?"

That was a good question, and no one had asked him before. Did he miss combat? The blazing hot, relentless heat? Being a stranger in a foreign land? Facing off with faceless assassins? No. But did he miss being part of something that big, fighting for the people who couldn't fight for themselves, wearing the uniform, earning the title of US marine? Hell yes. The answer was far too complicated for him to sort quickly, so he decided on the simplest truth. "I'm glad to be home."

"What was it like?" she asked.

He shrugged. Another question too complicated to answer thoroughly. "What's it like to be a single mom with a baby living alone out here?"

"Lonely," she said almost immediately, "and sometimes scary." She looked away, but the truth of the words was there in her soft voice.

Cade understood both answers quite well. "Same," he said.

Lyndy returned her gaze to him. "What about you? Any kids back in Lexington?"

"No." Cade took the seat beside hers. "I don't think having a family is in the cards for me. My father left a lot to be desired." He let a small smile form on his lips at the horrendous understatement and kicked himself mentally for oversharing. Normally he was notorious for one-word answers. Choosing to become Susie Chatterbox now, when he was supposed to be making a good first impression on a new client, was a huge error in judgment.

"He ruined the idea of family for you?" she guessed, tilting slightly forward, as if the answer mattered.

Cade considered the question. His father had ruined a lot of things for him, but not the desire to have a family. A real one. One that loved and supported one another. "I just think it's probably best I pass on the opportunity to share what I learned about parenting, which isn't much and none of which is good."

Lyndy's small mouth pulled down at the sides. "I'm sorry."

Cade's muscles stiffened. He took a deep drink of coffee and made solid plans to shut the hell up.

Lyndy sat straighter and rubbed the freckled skin beneath a wisp of pale blond bangs. "I should let you get settled. It's late and Gus is an early riser."

"Of course." Cade stood when she did and waited while she passed. "I'll be here if you need me."

He tried and failed to keep his eyes off her as she walked away. He imagined he wasn't the only man to feel that way, and a protective instinct tugged at his core.

She vanished a few steps later, and he released a heavy breath.

Maybe it was the fact she looked so small and vulnerable, or maybe it was the fact she was a new mother, but Cade's jaw locked at the memory of why he was there. Someone had tried to hurt her tonight.

He'd make darn sure that didn't happen again.

LYNDY DIDN'T SLEEP well despite her new home-security cowboy. She'd set up Gus's travel crib in her room, then shoved her tallest dresser in front of her window and her heaviest one in front of the locked bedroom door. Still, she'd remained awake most of the night.

Gus woke at two, then again at seven sharp.

She was waiting. Already dressed in her best-fitting jeans and a faded old T-shirt, she'd combed her hair and driven a lip gloss wand over her lips before she heard his first cry. A little mascara, and she was ready to face the day.

She changed Gus into his blue onesie covered in lassos, stretched a pair of faux jeans over his dimpled legs and diapered bottom, then brown socks, designed to look like little cowboy boots, over each chubby foot. Perfect. Adorable. *Safe.* She released a steadying breath with the final thought, then scooped him into her arms and crept down the hall to her kitchen, careful not to wake the man sleeping in her guest room.

The first rays of sunlight drifted through her French doors, warming the cool linoleum beneath her bare feet. Cheery red and green decor met her at every turn, an effort to make Gus's first holiday season magical. Thanksgiving had been a bust, but what could be expected with a single mom watching her figure and a baby on formula and pureed peas?

She strapped Gus into his highchair and gave the clear plastic snowman on his tray a playful shake. The toy wobbled without falling, stuck to the tray by a suction cup. Gus followed suit, giving the snowman a whack that rattled the tiny blue and white balls inside him.

Lyndy smiled. "I'll be right back with your bottle."

The patio door swung open as she pressed the brew button on her coffee maker, and Cade strode inside. She suspected the shock on his face rivaled the expression on her own. "I hope I didn't wake you," he said, stripping out of the wool-lined denim coat. He hung the jacket on the rack beside her French door and turned his Stetson upside down on the counter. The material of his pale gray T-shirt clung to the planes and angles of his chest and torso.

She hadn't dreamed it, as she'd suspected, or blown his attractiveness out of proportion as she'd tossed and turned through the night. Cade Lance was smoking hot. Which, in her experience, probably meant he knew it and was insufferable, or he didn't know it because he had the IQ of a potato.

"No," Lyndy said, refocusing on the coffee. "You startled me. I've been sneaking around in here trying not to wake you."

Cade moved in close and stretched an arm in her direction. "May I?" he asked reaching for the freshly brewed pot.

"Mmm-hmm." She moved away and finished making Gus's bottle.

He poured two mugs and offered one to her.

"Thanks." She carried it to the table along with Gus's bottle, then helped her son manage his breakfast. "How did you sleep?"

Cade leaned against the counter and crossed his long legs at the ankles. "I don't sleep."

"No?" She waited for more on the subject, but it didn't come, so she switched gears. "What were you doing outside?" she asked, still puzzling over the fact he didn't sleep. Was that by choice? Part of the job? Personally, she'd give anything for an uninterrupted eight hours.

"I patrolled the property. Evaluated the perimeter. Checked your barn and outbuildings."

Her stomach tightened with unbidden memories of the previous night and the life-changing knowledge of exactly who Cade had been looking for. "Find anything I should worry about?"

"Just a whole lot of quiet. It's a large property. Probably best if you stick close to the house. Stay in the yard. We need to establish a tight perimeter. Eight acres is too much to monitor with any real success." He ran a huge hand over his cropped hair.

Lyndy blew across the surface of her steaming coffee, enjoying the heady scent and the current view. If she had to be trapped inside with anyone, Cade certainly wasn't the worst she could do.

He dropped his hand away from his hair and jerked to attention, suddenly focused in the direction of her front door. "Wait here." He pushed away from the counter, revealing a holstered gun in the waistband of his jeans as he passed her.

Lyndy felt her eyes go wide. "What's happening?"

Cade was already at the front window. "Someone's here."

Lyndy forced herself upright, freeing Gus from his highchair and gripping him to her chest. A moment later, she heard tires crunching over her gravel drive. "Who is it?"

"Black SUV. Government plates." He relaxed visibly. "Feds."

"Feds?" she parroted, her voice hitching unnaturally. "Federal agents?"

He nodded. "It's protocol for the FBI to get involved when words like 'serial killer' start being thrown around."

Lyndy swallowed a brick of nausea and joined him at the door.

The world glistened outside beneath a layer of shimmering frost.

Detective Owens strode up the walk with a man in a black suit on his heels. They climbed the front porch steps in tandem, breaths coming in little white puffs. Cade opened the front door.

"Morning, Ms. Wells, Gus." Detective Owens smiled at her, then at her baby boy. "And this must be Cade Lance. It's nice to finally meet you."

Cade offered the detective his hand. "You, as well."

Lyndy cuddled Gus tighter, warming him against the chilly morning air. "Come in." She stepped back to make room for the men to pass, certain that whatever measure of peace she'd found over her first cup of coffee was soundly behind her. "How do you know each other?"

"I have a lot of family in law enforcement throughout the state," Cade said, closing the door behind her guests.

The suit offered Cade a hand before shaking hers, as well. "I'm Agent Maxwell. Sorry to show up so early and unannounced. We felt that time was of the essence. You understand."

She nodded woodenly, though she didn't understand any of it. The previous night had been a blur, and by the light of day, the memories felt more like something she'd seen in a movie than something she'd truly experienced. If it wasn't for the scrapes and bruises on her body and the men before her, she'd question if any of it was real.

The living room felt infinitely smaller with three

tightly wound men gathered inside. Agent Maxwell and Detective Owens took seats on opposite ends of her couch. Cade chose the love seat beside it, and after a moment of indecision, Lyndy took Gus with her to the armchair between the two. The apex, it seemed, of a brooding triangle.

Detective Owens cleared his throat and offered Lyndy an encouraging smile. "How are you feeling this morning?"

"I'm okay," she said, repositioning Gus in her arms. "I think we're going to be just fine." That was the prayer anyway, and she had Cade now. Presumably her attacker would move on, and there was still a significant possibility that he wasn't the serial killer they suspected he might be. What were they going on, really? Didn't every abduction happen like hers? A woman alone at dusk. A man creeping in the shadows? She shivered as a memory of her escape thrust itself forward.

"Have you thought of anything more you can tell us?" Detective Owens asked. "Anything at all. Even something that seems insignificant to you might be the exact detail the FBI needs to decide where to go next."

"No." She shook her head. Lyndy had replayed the attack a thousand times, but nothing ever changed. "Nothing new."

Cade leaned forward, drawing Lyndy's attention and fixing his gaze on Agent Maxwell. "What can you tell us about her attacker?"

The agent studied Cade for a long moment before shifting his gaze to Lyndy. "We believe you were targeted by a man we're calling the Kentucky Tom Cat because he likes to play cat and mouse with his victims. So far, more than a dozen women in surrounding counties have reported experiences exactly like yours. He hides in the shadows near their cars or outside their front doors and waits for them to come near. He dresses in dark coveralls. Only whispers. Always wears gloves. He's very methodical in the care he takes to repeat his crimes and hide his identity."

The moments of her near abduction returned with a vivid and visceral crash. She touched the heated skin of her throat, reminding herself the assailant's arm was no longer there. It was just a memory. She could breathe. She was safe.

She felt Cade's gaze on her cheek but couldn't bring herself to look at him.

"You say he repeats the crimes?" Cade asked. "What are the details?"

"Truthfully," Detective Owens answered, "the crimes have escalated."

Agent Maxwell shot the detective a warning look. Clearly this was his information to divulge. "Two of the early victims were abducted, beaten, raped and eventually released, though none could describe their attacker and there was no DNA evidence left behind. The four most recent victims were killed," he said flatly. "Our profiler believes the Tom Cat was probably practicing early on, deciding how he wanted the scenarios to play out."

"What kind of man are we looking for?" Cade asked. "What's the physical profile?"

"White," the agent said, "in his thirties, white collar, acceptably attractive and comfortable enough interacting with people that he wouldn't stand out as dangerous." He turned his eyes to Lyndy. "We believe you probably know him. He's been in your life somehow before this and taken his time to learn your routines and patterns."

Lyndy's chest tightened, and she struggled to take a full breath. "What about the other women? You said they're from other counties, but I never leave town. Did he know all of us?"

"We believe so, yes. He likely has a job that allows or requires him to travel regularly, at least within the tri-county area."

"And he's killed four women?" she asked, feeling the coffee churn in her empty stomach.

"Four that we're aware of. There could be more, but because the deaths were in different counties, and there were a number of months between the discovery of each body, it took some time to put the crimes together, then a little longer to find and interview victims of the earlier crimes we now believe he was responsible for."

A renegade tear trailed over Lyndy's cheek, hot and unbidden. She swiped it away, desperate to appear much stronger than she was for the sake of her company. Three men who'd probably never known the bone-deep, blood-freezing terror of being over-powered the way she had been.

"Ms. Wells?" the agent asked. "If you'd like to stop…"

"No. I want to get through this. It's just that I can still feel his hands on me." She swallowed another massive lump of fear and grimaced at the ache.

To her surprise, Cade covered her small hand with his and gave her fingers a squeeze. She turned to find determination in his fierce blue eyes.

Her jaw dropped, and he released her, as if the comforting gesture and encouraging words were nothing remarkable. As if he, one of three virtual strangers in the room, hadn't noticed she was on the verge of a freak-out, then delivered the perfect antidote.

Lyndy kissed Gus's soft hair to re-center herself, then asked the question that had kept her up all night. "Why is he doing this?"

The agent pursed his lips and folded his hands on his lap before answering. "It could be a number of things. Perhaps the result of severe neglect or abuse as a child. Maybe he's off his meds or desperately in need of them. We won't know for sure until we can talk to him. Maybe not even then. First, we have to figure out who he is. We're reviewing footage from the news coverage at your crime scene. The seg-ment drew a crowd. If the Tom Cat enjoys the spot-light, he might be on the tape, eating up the hoopla.

We're also paying close attention to all the anonymous tips that come in. Sometimes guys like this will try to get involved in their own investigations, become informants, insert themselves however they can. Some want to be caught. Others want to up the stakes. We suspect the Tom Cat enjoys the hunt as much as the attack. Maybe more. He seems to put extreme thought into choosing his victims and acting on the plans."

Cade rubbed a hand over his lips, apparently processing the horror only a little better than she was. "One more question," he said. "I'm still unclear why you think Ms. Wells's attacker is the same man you're describing? Is it just because he was near her car after dark?"

"I'm afraid not," Agent Maxwell said solemnly. He opened a black leather portfolio and retrieved a stack of glossy eight-by-ten photos. He began to place them in rows across the coffee table.

Cade swore under his breath, and Detective Owens looked away.

Lyndy's lungs, eyes and nose burned as she watched photo after photo appear in the surreal lineup of the Tom Cat's victims. More than sixteen in all, each one abducted, *four killed*.

And every victim looked exactly like Lyndy.

Chapter Three

It was hours after the detective and agent left before Cade dared approach Lyndy's bedroom door. She'd taken Gus and gone straight into her room before the federal agent's SUV had made it out of the driveway. Cade had spent the meantime replacing all the old locks on her farmhouse doors and windows. He'd passed by her closed bedroom door a few times, as well, unsure if he should check on her or leave her alone. It was always quiet. Maybe she'd fallen asleep with her baby? Maybe she was on a private phone call, or was crying. How could he know? Was it his job to know? Possibly, but it was definitely not his job to intrude on her personal space. She'd clearly shut the door for privacy. In all his previous jobs, the client had gone on with his or her life while Cade simply tagged along, keeping an eye out, blending into the background while abusive exes or second-rate stalkers were located and arrested in a timely manner. He'd never been assigned to someone whose life had been essentially and indefinitely put on hold by anything so serious. The situation had him on edge. He couldn't imagine what someone half his size with none of his training and an infant to protect might be feeling.

When she hadn't made a reappearance by lunch, Cade made a new plan. He prepared a stack of sandwiches from the meats and cheeses in her fridge and poured two glasses of ice water, then rapped gently on her door. "Hello?"

He waited through the squeaky sound of bedsprings and the featherlight pats of Lyndy's feet over wooden floorboards. He prepared himself for the worst. For a woman with frayed nerves. A woman in tears. A combination of the two?

Lyndy opened the door looking like his favorite daydream. She'd added waves to her short blond hair and traded the T-shirt and jeans for a creamy V-neck sweater and brown leggings that highlighted her curves and drew his attention inappropriately. She'd paired the flirty little ensemble with tan-and-white cowgirl boots.

"Hey," she said, her big blue eyes wide and alert. "I've been thinking, and I want to help find this guy, who I'm going to call Tom, because I refuse to call any adult person *the Tom Cat*."

Cade forced his eyes away from her clingy cashmere top only to find his gaze stuck to the iridescent coating of gloss on her perfect rosebud mouth. "Okay."

"Great." She slipped past him and headed for the

kitchen with a swing in her hips. "What did you do while you were in the Marines?"

He did his best to keep his eyes off her backside as she moved to the table and helped herself to half a sandwich. "What do you mean?"

She took a bite and chewed thoughtfully. "This is delicious. Thank you. I meant, what was your job? Were you a mechanic? A medic? A sharpshooter?"

"No." But he was one hell of a shot. "I was in Intelligence."

Her eyes lit. "So you're observant."

Painfully so, he thought, shifting uncomfortably in his jeans. "Why?"

Lyndy gave her sandwich a rest and bit into the thick of her bottom lip. "I thought we could take Gus into town and visit the places I go most frequently, aside from the office. I called off work for the rest of the week. I don't want to get into all this with my coworkers just yet."

"You want me to take you into town so you can show me around?" he asked, unsure of her angle.

"Yeah." A slight look of guilt crossed her pretty face. "I pulled up the social media profiles of the four fatal Tom Cat victims while I was in my room."

Cade groaned.

Lyndy pressed on. "I want to know how Tom found me and how he found them. There has to be a common denominator. Sure, we look alike, but what put us in his path? Did he just drive around looking for short blondes with bobbed hair, blue eyes and freckles?" She huffed. "I can't figure it out, but I was never in Intelligence." Her eyes flashed. "Maybe you'll notice something I haven't."

Cade crossed his arms and stared. He didn't like the idea of leaving the house with her, not when the man who attacked her was still out there. And he hated the idea of her getting any more involved in this mess than she already was. "I think we should let the feds and Owens handle the investigation. They'll do their jobs and I'll do mine. You'll be easier to defend at a secure location. If you think of anything new you want to tell them, you can give them a call."

Her brows furrowed. "Well, I can't stay in here until they find him. It's already been a year since his first murder and there were plenty of victims before those, plus I hate being idle." Lyndy pursed her lips. "I'm scared, and I have to do something."

"Why don't I help you put up the Christmas tree? Maybe hang some stockings?" He tipped his head in the direction of a stack of plastic storage bins lined against the living room wall. She'd clearly been planning to decorate soon. Why not today? "I'll make hot chocolate."

She crossed her arms, unmoved and mimicking his stance. "I want to help catch this guy before he strikes again. What if he's planning his next attack now? What if I'm not so lucky the next time? What if he hurts Gus? Or another woman? The more input I can give the police, the faster this lunatic can be caught, and the sooner I can sleep again. Preferably before Christmas."

Cade moved his hands to his hips. He couldn't hold her captive or tell her what to do, but he could stick close, and he could keep her safe. "All right," he conceded, "but you have to stay in my sights at all times, preferably within reach, and if I say it's time to go, we need to leave immediately."

She nodded. "Agreed," she said. "And I think we should pretend to be a couple." She raised a palm. "Hear me out."

Cade worked to control his stunned expression. He'd endured some wild requests from clients before, but those usually involved him staying out of the way, not faking a romantic relationship. And from an ethical and professional standpoint, given the physical effect this woman was having on him from the start, he should definitely say no.

"Sometimes having a boyfriend is the only thing that gets creeps to leave women alone," Lyndy said, sounding as if she'd had some solid personal experience on the subject.

He ground his teeth at the thought of someone not accepting her rejection immediately and with an apology.

"According to the other victims' social media statuses," she continued, "they were all single. Maybe if I have a significant other, it will diminish his interest in me while we look for where he and I might have initially crossed paths. I'm not suggesting anything inappropriate," she said, clearly on a roll. "You don't have to kiss me or anything. Just some hand-holding or close walking while we're in public. I wasn't asking you to…" She motioned between them until her cheeks went red. "Never mind. Forget I suggested it."

Cade laughed, then frowned. Pretending to be her boyfriend, for her safety's sake, sounded like just enough fun to cause him trouble later. Though he wasn't ready to think too long or hard about how much or what kind of trouble. What worried him more was the fact he couldn't say no to her. *He didn't want to.* If walking through town made her feel like she was helping save other women, if it made her happy, then they were going to town. "How long have we been dating?"

Lyndy rocked onto her toes and beamed; a flush of gratitude and appreciation colored her cheeks and flooded her eyes. "Not long," she said. "The relationship's still new, so we're gooey on each other. That'll keep me close to you, and explain why we don't know everything about one another in case anyone asks questions. I'll get Gus." She hurried away, the soft material of her leggings caressing the curve of her backside.

Cade let his head fall back and his lids go shut. He swallowed an internal groan. If she kept looking at him like that, he wouldn't be able to concentrate long enough to spot a charging rhino before it hit her, and that was the absolute scariest thought he'd had since leaving Afghanistan.

LYNDY KEPT HER eyes on the scenery as they rode into downtown Piedmont. Her nerves were shot. Her bravado had failed, and she was certain that going home might actually be the smartest thing she could do. Instead, she'd soon be strolling around town with Gus and a man wearing a cowboy hat and blue jeans that made her think anything was possible. Plus a few other things she hadn't thought about in a year. She blamed the lapse of judgment on discovering her favorite clothes fitted again and the unfounded confidence that came with wearing them.

Beyond the glass, her town had openly welcomed the holiday season. Shops had dragged faux snowmen and artificial decorated trees outside their doors. Oversize wreaths hung from lampposts and familiar Christmas tunes piped through hidden speakers on the more highly trafficked streets. "Here." She pointed to a small lot between brick office buildings. "We can park for free as long as we don't stay more than two hours."

Cade maneuvered his mammoth truck into a tiny space and cut the engine. "Are you sure you feel up to this?"

"No," she answered honestly, "but I'm sure the potential payoff is worth a walk through town on a beautiful day. Don't you agree?" She unfastened her seat belt and pulled her purse onto her lap.

Cade watched her with knowing eyes, and she forced herself not to squirm. He probably saw everything she didn't say. He probably knew she was a coward playing at brave. That she'd spent an hour checking the prices on monthlong cruises to Alaska and bus fare to Timbuktu before deciding to suck it up and become part of the solution.

She worked her dry mouth open and pulled in a steadying breath. "We'll be quick. Then we can go home and look over the other women's online profiles and photos again. See if anything matches." Lyndy glanced at Gus in his car seat on the rear bench, then back at Cade. "Let me know if you notice any man watching me."

Cade made a sour face and turned away. "With you wearing that outfit, I'm going to need to make a list," he mumbled, climbing out the driver's side door.

Lyndy smiled. It really was a great outfit.

She joined Cade on the sidewalk and tucked Gus into the sling she used to keep him on her hip when he was alert and eager to explore. The sling had been made for her and fitted nicely over the white waist-length ski jacket she'd paired with her ensemble. "So, this is our big town," she told Cade with a grin. "It's no Lexington, but it's got everything a person could want."

Cade moved in close to her side and slid his palm against hers. "Agreed." He twined their fingers and gave hers a squeeze. "Are we still doing this?"

Lyndy opened her mouth, then shut it. The unexpected pulse of electricity beating through their joined hands and in her chest was a whole lot to process. "Um." She cleared her throat. "We don't have to."

"Does it make you feel safer?" he asked.

"Yes," she answered, more breathlessly than intended and curled her fingers over his.

An hour later they'd visited a dozen places she loved to go. She'd never realized how many locations she stopped on a regular basis. Bank, post office, general shopping, ice cream…the list went on. And they hadn't even gotten to the gym.

They headed up the street to Lyndy's favorite café and climbed the steps to the door. "Have you seen anything interesting yet?" she asked. "Anything unusual?"

"I saw you dig a pacifier from the bottom of your purse and clean it with your mouth before giving it to your kid," he said. "That was weird."

"It was dirty." She rubbed goose bumps off the back of her neck while Cade opened the door for her, then she moved swiftly inside. For the first time all day, she felt strangely exposed. Lyndy gave the street outside a cursory glance. Nothing seemed out of place to her. No creepy figures glaring back. Maybe she was just running out of steam.

"You okay?" Cade asked, setting his palm against her back.

"Yeah." She gave him a small smile. "I'm definitely disappointed nothing stood out during our walk, but uneventful seems pretty good, too."

He nodded but cast his gaze in the direction she'd just looked. Had he sensed something too, or was he that in tune with her somehow? "Where do we go from here?" he asked.

"I'm not sure." She stroked Gus's cheek and led Cade to a corner table. "According to their social media accounts, the other victims worked in offices just like mine."

"What do you do in your office?" he asked.

"Interviews, mostly. I work at a local temping agency, placing folks into roles where companies have needs. We work with businesses in Piedmont and throughout northern Kentucky. Sometimes as far as Cincinnati, Ohio, but none in any of the towns where Tom's other victims were found. I checked."

He smiled. "Of course you did."

LYNDY IGNORED THE note of pride in his tone and the corresponding bolt of warmth in her core. "As far as I can tell, none of the other women had babies. Do you think Tom found me at my ob-gyn or Lamaze classes? Do you think he has my home address?" She ran a nervous hand through her hair and looked outside once more.

Cade captured her hand in his and tugged gently until she looked his way. "Hey." He stroked his broad thumb across the back of her fingers. "I've got you," he said slow and smooth. The sexy tenor of his voice mixed with the scent of his cologne and curled her toes inside her boots.

Another wave of eerie goose bumps hit, and she turned her face back to the window.

"What is it?" Cade asked, stepping forward and staring through the glass at her side. "Do you see something?"

"No. I just have this icky feeling."

The waitress appeared. "What can I get started for you guys?"

Lyndy's stomach coiled, and the fine hairs on her arms rose to attention beneath her coat and sweater. "A latte for me, please," she told the young girl with a brown corkscrew ponytail and white apron. She touched Cade's arm, reluctantly dragging his gaze from the window. "I should change Gus. I'll be right back."

Cade looked over her shoulder toward the bathroom hallway. "All right."

The waitress waited, impatiently. "For you, sir?"

Lyndy hustled to the ladies' room without waiting to hear his order. She needed to put some distance between herself and the picture window overlooking Main Street, then hopefully shake off the heebie-jeebies crawling all over her skin. When she got back to Cade, she was going to suggest they take their orders *to go*.

CADE ORDERED A house coffee and took the corner seat where he could easily watch the street, the café patrons and the hallway where Lyndy and her son had run off. Until a minute ago, the day had been peaceful, and he'd enjoyed the walk around a relatively quiet town. Being with Lyndy and her son felt incredibly normal and inexplicably calming. It was a welcome change after the last few years spent on edge. Cade had even dared to hope the FBI agent was wrong, and Lyndy's experience wasn't part of this chain of escalating attacks, but the way she'd looked outside before taking off said otherwise. Cade had learned long ago to trust his gut. Now he was going to trust hers.

The familiar bong of a special news bulletin brought his attention to the television hanging behind the register. A woman with a mic and pantsuit centered the screen outside a park. A thick line of text below her read, *Kentucky Tom Cat Killer comes a little too close for comfort.*

Cade focused on the gathered crowd. What if Lyndy's attacker was on-screen right now? The camera maintained a tight focus on the reporter, blurring onlookers' faces. Still, there were other things worth noting. A large red pickup truck in the background, for example, and a man dressed in all camouflage on the periphery.

Cade scanned the café and then the street. No activity in the bathroom hallway. No one in full camouflage. No red pickups outside. Though there was a man in a plain black ball cap across the street about a block away, and there had been one just like that on television until the news clip ended. The cap had belonged to one of the many blurred faces.

Cade stood for a better look at the man outside, but distance and a shadow cast from a nearby building made it nearly impossible to discern anything specific about him. He leaned against a telephone pole with his back to the street, but he'd looked over his shoulder several times since Cade had begun to watch. A coincidence? Something more sinister? Maybe he was just a man waiting for his friends or a spouse. The ball cap was nothing special, after all. Lots of people owned plain black caps, though he was the only one in the immediate area.

The bathroom door opened, and Lyndy strode out. Her smile was bright and wide as she kissed her baby's little fingers. "Sorry that took so long. This little guy thought it was playtime." Her smile fell. "What's wrong?"

Cade glanced back across the street, but the man was gone. "I'm not sure," he said. Cade rubbed his chin as an interesting idea formed. "Agent Maxwell said Tom might be watching the crime scenes, and I can't help wondering if he's also watching you."

Lyndy stilled. "I wondered that, too." She wound her arm around his and moved in close. Her soft, honey-scented skin was a distraction Cade couldn't afford, but that was a whole other problem.

"There was someone up the block a minute ago," he said. "He seemed to be looking this way, but I took my eyes off of him, and now he's gone." He checked every face on the street for one that was staring back, checked every head for the simple black cap, but found none.

"Do you think he's gone?" she asked. "Or just

moved out of sight?" Lyndy slid her hand down his forearm and twined her shaking fingers with his.

"I don't know," Cade admitted. *But there was one way to tell.*

He dipped his head slightly and turned to face Lyndy, forming a small cocoon between them where the conversation would be for their ears only. "I'd like to test a theory," he began carefully. "It could help us know if someone's still watching."

Lyndy glanced outside, then back to Cade. "Okay."

He ran his hands along her arms to her elbows. "Are you comfortable with me kissing your cheek?"

She nodded, a sudden storm brewing in her eyes.

"At this angle it will look like something more from outside. Ready?"

Lyndy wet her lips. "Yes."

"First, laugh," he whispered. "Pretend I've said something that makes you really happy."

Lyndy's worried expression softened into a warm smile and a bubble of tinkling laughter slipped out.

The sound burrowed deep into Cade's core, and he slid his palm against her soft cheek. He tucked a swath of short hair gently behind her ear, and Lyndy's expression changed again.

She covered his hand with hers and pressed his palm more firmly to her cheek before rising onto her toes and angling her beautiful face up to his.

Her glossy lips parted, and her eyelids drifted shut.

Cade fought the urge to take her mouth and taste those sweet lips as her breath danced over his skin.

She curved her small hand around the nape of his neck and pulled him in closer. "How's this instead?" she whispered.

BOOM! The sudden sound of an explosion tore them apart.

The formerly crystal clear café window was now nothing more than a million tiny shards of glass. A gust of icy wind swirled through the café and down Cade's spine.

Undeniably, the Kentucky Tom Cat Killer was still hunting his mouse.

Chapter Four

Cade took the turn away from town at a crawl, half his attention on Lyndy and half on the road ahead. "You okay?" he asked, for at least the dozenth time since witnessing the café window shatter beside him.

If Cade had to guess, he'd say the culprit used a glass punch to destroy the window. He'd seen the tool used before with similar results, though never on such a large pane. It was generally used by emergency personnel to save pets or children locked in cars on hot days or free the passengers of vehicles that had become submerged, but could be effective under any circumstance. Not to mention easy to acquire and operate. Also, small and easily concealed.

Cade's grip tightened on the wheel as the reality hit home once more. The Kentucky Tom Cat Killer was still watching Lyndy. Cade couldn't help wondering what else the psychopath had in his arsenal. Or what he would do to Lyndy if Cade failed.

Lyndy dragged her attention away from the collection of lawmen shrinking behind them in the distance, uselessly littering the sidewalk drenched in broken glass. Their diminishing silhouettes reflected in the rearview mirror and the ones on the sides. "I'm still okay," she said, her eyes clear and voice steady, before turning back to her window.

She'd been equally calm as she'd given her statement to the police and listened to the statements of others standing nearby. Nearly two dozen people had heard the window break. No one had seen who'd caused it.

And Cade hadn't seen the man in the black ball cap again.

He gave Lyndy another look. She seemed fine, sounded fine, looked fantastic, but how could she be any of those things? A serial killer had recently tried and failed to abduct her and her infant son. Now the lunatic was stalking her. He didn't need an eyewitness to confirm that truth. They'd agreed to test the theory, and they'd gotten their answer loud and clear when she'd risen on her toes to kiss him. The window hadn't exploded on its own. The Tom Cat had been watching, and he'd done what it took to stop the kiss.

But why had Lyndy been about to kiss him on the lips when Cade had just explained that a kiss on her cheek would do the trick? He slid his eyes in her direction once more. Did she want to kiss him? The possibility was nearly as jarring as the effort's aftermath. He shook the thought away. They'd just met. She was in danger. People did crazy things under difficult circumstances. He cleared his throat and refocused his thoughts on something sensible. "You don't have to put up a brave front," he said. "The situation you're in would wreck anyone."

"I'm not wrecked," she said defiantly, "and I do have to put up a front. If not for Gus, then for effect." She turned to him suddenly, imploring him with those wide blue eyes. "I'm terrified. My insides are in knots and my hands are trembling, but I can't let whoever is doing this know he's getting exactly what he wants. He doesn't deserve that. And to be honest, if I let myself start crying now, I probably won't stop, so it's better that I just schedule my complete emotional breakdown for another time, I think."

Cade felt the corners of his mouth edge up, impressed with her humor and fortitude despite it all. Though he knew the words she'd spoken in jest were likely true. He'd thought a number of similar things in bad situations. There was a time to fight and a time to let go. Clearly it was still time to fight.

"Do you think he did it to stop the kiss or to let me know he's still here?" Lyndy asked, pulling Cade's attention once more. "Is it a game to him? Or was it a power move?"

"Maybe both," Cade answered honestly. "I've never studied serial killers, but this feels more serious than a game to me." In truth, whatever this was felt more like a hunt.

Lyndy wet her pink lips and exhaled long and slow. "Great."

Cade signaled his next turn, then cast a careful look at the petite blonde beside him. "I might've made it worse by showing up. Not that you had a choice. You obviously need the protection, but I'm willing to bet the nut doesn't appreciate the competition."

She turned to him at the word *competition*, eyes wide in understanding. "I'll be harder to take now. We've inadvertently upped the stakes."

Cade turned his attention back to the road. "I will protect you," he vowed. "You and Gus. You can count on that. It's what I'm trained for."

"Protected a lot of helpless victims?" she asked, self-deprecation thick in her tone.

"Yes." *Entire towns full*, he thought sadly. "But you aren't helpless. You've already fought and won against this guy once. Don't forget that. You're the victor here. He's the loser."

Her crystal eyes brimmed with unshed tears as she shifted on the seat, angling her body toward him. Her sweet honey scent wafted through the warming cab. "It was still a good idea to try to draw him out," she said. "Even if the authorities don't catch him today, at least we've confirmed he's still here. The feds won't leave now, and the story will be all over the news. Everyone will know about him, and that'll make them safer. Plus, he'll be forced to move carefully. All good things."

That was all true, but he hadn't expected her concern about the town to warm him to her further. He cleared his throat and attempted to get mentally back on course. "The police presence definitely drew a big crowd. Lots of faces to compare with those in the news footage shot outside the park following your attack. I'm sure it won't be long before officials have the Tom Cat in their crosshairs."

Lyndy settled back in her seat once more, a grin on her pretty lips. "Then we really did do a good thing. I heard the detective say they were opening a tip line, too."

"Tip lines can be complicated," Cade said, taking the final turn onto Lyndy's road. "Those numbers generally bring out half the nutjobs and attention seekers in the county."

"Isn't that what Tom is?" she asked. "A nutjob and attention seeker? Maybe he'll call in."

Cade cocked an eyebrow. "Why does this awful conversation seem to make you happy?"

"Because I'm doing something, even if it's only brainstorming. I can't sit idle and be a duck."

"A duck?"

She rolled her eyes and turned away once more. "A sitting duck."

"Right." Cade shook his head, strangely proud of her go-getter attitude. Guarding this blond beauty and her infant son would be more complicated than he'd originally bargained.

But Cade was up for the challenge.

LYNDY SETTLED GUS into his crib for a nap, then went to hunt down some sweet tea. The drink jazzed a lot of folks up, too much sugar and caffeine, but the combination was balm to her jagged nerves. Her mother and grandmother had poured sweet tea for every occasion, whether they'd needed to talk, laugh or cry. These days, the mere scent of it tossed her into fits of nostalgia, but for a long time after each of their deaths, the scent had pushed her to tears. At the moment, she needed a tall, cold glass to remind her she would get through this, the way she'd gotten through their losses, Sam's and everything else life had unfairly thrown at her.

She sighed at the blessed sight of a nearly full pitcher in her refrigerator, then poured two Mason jars full when she caught sight of Cade, making his way across the property outside the kitchen window. His steady gaze jumped to meet hers in the window above the sink and his scowl seemed to fade.

"Sweet tea?" she asked, projecting her voice and lifting a jar into Cade's view.

He cleared the back porch steps with an effortless leap, then crossed into the kitchen a moment later. "I love sweet tea." He set his hat on the counter and accepted the jar. His lips curved into a smile as he sipped. "That's good."

"Thanks. It's my grandmama's recipe. According to her this tea could fix anything that ails ya." Lyndy returned his smile. "I'm not sure how well it'll work on fending off serial killers, but I'm willing to give it a try." She raised the jar to her lips, a fresh ribbon of fear tightening around her heart.

Cade moved into the space beside her, leaning against the sink and sipping his tea. "You've got a nice place here."

"Thanks." She breathed in the calm radiating from him and prayed the tea would do its work.

"I'm truly sorry you lost your fiancé like that. I'm sorry Gus lost his daddy."

Lyndy's heart wrenched at the kindness spoken toward her son, and at the reminder that her boy, like her, would grow up without a father. It wasn't what she'd want for anyone, certainly not for her own child, but here she was. Her father had left by choice. Gus's had been taken. A vicious cycle of loss.

"They never got to meet," she said, her grandmama's tea making the story a little easier to tell. "I couldn't eat or sleep for days after Sam died. I was sick all the time, and I'd assumed it was shock. It was morning sickness, but I didn't know. I was too mired in grief to realize he'd left me with a new life."

Cade watched her. "Sam never knew?"

"No." She turned the cold jar in her hands, letting cool drops of condensation roll over her fingers.

"How long has he been gone?"

"A year." She pulled in a long breath, then released it slowly, the way she'd learned at her support group for victims of sudden loss. "Somedays the memories feel more like bits from movies I've almost forgotten than reality." She puffed out her cheeks and let her eyes fall shut. Just like the memories of her attack. Her brain's way of dealing with the trauma. "Sorry." She shot him an impish smile. "Talk about oversharing."

"It's not," Cade assured. "I want to know, and what you're describing is typical in the aftermath of trauma. My time spent overseas feels like that to me sometimes. I know I was there. Know I saw and experienced certain things, but my mind puts a filter on them for distance. It cushions the impact, and I don't always mind. There was a time when those cushions kept me moving forward."

Lyndy finished her tea and set the jar aside, enjoying the companionable silence that followed. "We might be kindred spirits, Cade Lance."

"We might," he agreed.

Lyndy felt the brush of his arm against hers as they stood side by side in her kitchen. The musky scent of him warmed her, and she leaned closer, hungry for more of whatever it was about him that made her feel so safe. So strong. And so insanely feminine. She did her best to remember their relationship was professional. That she'd hired him to protect her and her son. And that it would be reckless and stupid to read into anything he said or did as attraction to her. Still, she enjoyed the strange stirring his nearness created in her. And she didn't mind the distraction.

Cade turned toward her, eyebrows drawn, as if he'd somehow read her mind. "Lyndy?"

She bit into her bottom lip, reminding herself that she needed Cade for protection, and that she wasn't in the market for a man. For the next eighteen years or so Gus would come before everything else, her hormones included. "Yes?"

Curiosity danced in his narrowed eyes. "In the café today…what were you planning on doing before the glass broke?"

She stared dumbly back, unable to admit she'd planned to kiss him. That she'd been caught in the moment, trapped in his spell, and it had felt like the exact right thing to do.

Until it hadn't.

Cade's lips parted, and his gaze fell to her mouth.

She imagined the taste of him. The warmth and pressure of his tongue on hers. The delicious scrape of his unshaven cheek against her skin.

Gus's angry cry ricocheted through her home and heart, throwing ice onto her fire and embarrassing her to the core. She jumped away, unable to look at Cade as she dashed down the hall toward Gus's room.

She had no idea what was wrong with her, but one thing was for sure.

If she kept behaving like that, the Tom Cat wouldn't have a chance to kill her. She'd already be dead of humiliation.

Chapter Five

Cade spent the rest of the afternoon alone. Lyndy had only returned once from the bedroom. She made a bottle with Gus on one hip, poured another jar of iced tea, then vanished back down the hall, leaving Cade to himself. He hadn't minded the silence at first. He'd been wholly thankful, in fact, for the break that allowed him to collect his wits and breathe again without her presence skewing his thoughts.

He'd expected a logical explanation for her behavior at the café. Perhaps it was an off-the-cuff improvisation. Something she'd thought would be more effective in drawing Tom out than a peck on the cheek. Cade had been certain that Lyndy would answer with her usual directness and the same matter-of-fact attitude he'd come to appreciate. But instead, it had looked as if she wanted to kiss him again! Could that be right?

Either way, it left a more dangerous and pressing question unanswered. What would Cade have done if Gus hadn't broken the spell? The *correct* answer was that he would have pulled back and stopped her. He should have been prepared to explain politely that their relationship was professional. But before her son had uttered a peep, Cade had already imagined the weight of her against him as he curled her in his arms. He'd anticipated the press of her lips on his and the soft skim of her fingers against his chest.

UNABLE TO MAKE sense of the emotional collision, he'd decided to double down on the job at hand. First by walking a sensible perimeter around Lyndy's farmhouse and evaluating various access points. Then by checking his messages and the local news sites for updates on law enforcement's progress on the case. He started with a cup of coffee and his laptop, intending to search the headlines for details on the Kentucky Tom Cat. Instead, he found himself typing Lyndy's fiancé's name into the search engine.

The story of his tragic death had dominated headlines for days, but Cade was oddly curious about who Sam had been in life. He quickly learned that Sam had held down a sensible office job and volunteered at the county animal shelter. He'd played baseball on a community league and judged the annual children's fishing tournament. Sam's life had been wholesome to the extreme, and comparatively, Cade's life was a hot, sometimes dangerous, mess.

He clicked the link below a photo of Sam and Lyndy in the next set of search results and landed on her neglected social media page. The only update she'd made in weeks was to showcase Gus's smile. He frowned at a photo of Sam. The man's appearance was average in every possible way, from his nondescript khakis to his bland, neutral-colored polos. He'd worn white sneakers and the same haircut Cade had stopped accepting in middle school. Furthermore, Sam was painfully clean-shaven in every photo on her page, and had an air of purity and innocence Cade couldn't fully understand. No wonder Lyndy had loved him. Sam appeared to be everything Cade's father had never been and everything Cade wasn't. Everything a son needed.

He shut the laptop and went to refill his mug. Sam had been Mr. Perfect, but if Lyndy was ever in the market for a man with limited money, a jacked-up biological family and a questionable past, Cade was the guy for her. He'd gone to the military instead of college. His brothers-in-arms were his family. He'd die of boredom behind any desk, and he sure as hell didn't own a pair of khakis. Though he did have a few black Fortress Defense polos, if she was into that.

He laughed at the ridiculousness of his thoughts as he rifled through her kitchen in search of a nine-by-thirteen pan and a few chicken breasts. He needed to get his head on straight. Sure, Lyndy was beautiful, kind and fierce, but that didn't mean he had to start wondering if he was good enough for her. He was there as her bodyguard.

He set the oven to preheat, then grabbed his

phone. He needed to let his team know how the job was going and see if they had any advice for securing the vast perimeter.

His ears pricked at the sound of running water as he dialed. Bath time for baby? Or shower time for mama? Cade swallowed a groan, then stepped onto the frigid rear deck to wait for his call to connect.

If Lyndy was getting into the shower, he'd need plenty of fresh air to combat that image.

LYNDY ADJUSTED THE bathwater for Gus, losing herself in mommy mode, thankful for Gus's perfect, or possibly terrible, timing. Either way, she'd needed the reminder that her desires came second now. Gus would always be first. Bathed and changed, he now sat contentedly in his playpen while she opted to follow his lead with the cleanup. She tossed the soft sweater and leggings, gathered her barrel curls into a ponytail, then adjusted the water to her preference. Maybe a hot shower would keep her from trying to attack her protective detail for a third time today. She blushed, recalling the absurdity of her behavior. Clearly, it had been too long since anyone had looked at her the way Cade did. *Then again*, she thought, *no one has ever looked at me the way he does*. And looking at him did pretty thrilling things to her, too.

Twenty minutes later, she dried and dressed in her favorite jeans and a faded blue T-shirt, and then added fuzzy socks. She returned to Gus feeling more like herself than she had in a year, maybe longer.

"What do you think?" she asked her baby. "Snack time?"

Gus opened his mouth in a broad toothless grin that melted her heart, and she scooped him against her. "I love you," she sighed, cradling his warmth to her chest and treasuring the feel of him in her arms. "You will always be my number one guy. Even when you're big enough to carry me instead." Assuming she survived the looming serial killer and lived to see Gus grow up at all.

The ugly thought ruined her moment and sent a round of chills skittering down her spine. Her gaze snapped to the windows, laden with shadow, then to the closed bedroom door. Much as she'd tried to avoid Cade after her infinitely lame attempt to kiss him, again, she suddenly needed to see him more than she needed to protect her pride.

She hurried down the hall toward the sound of his strong and steady voice, thankful not to be alone. She owed Detective Owens and his wife a casserole and all her gratitude for sending Cade her way. She couldn't imagine what the nights would be like without him here to protect her. Heck, without him, she wouldn't even know she was still a target. And that would've only ended one way. She cringed at the thought.

"You'd like her," he said to whoever was on the other end of the call. "She's brave. She's got that mama-bear vibe."

Lyndy paused. Was he talking about her? The

mama bear reference was true enough, but how had he gotten the impression she was brave? She'd practically spent every moment since her near abduction fighting tears.

"Nah, I've got this," he went on, "but I could use some input on the perimeter situation and feedback on the pics and files I sent to your Fortress email account. Property details and county auditor information on the surrounding lands."

Lyndy stopped at the end of the hall, unsure how to announce her arrival and admiring the contours of his muscular back beneath the pale gray shirt.

He raked a hand over the top of his short hair, and her gaze lifted to his curled biceps. "Nah. I'm good. She's not what I expected. That's all."

She could only imagine what that meant. His tone implied the situation wasn't anything good, and she instantly regretted thinking the electricity she felt was mutual.

Gus cooed and gurgled, changing her train of thought from one of self-pity to panic.

Cade spun in their direction before Lyndy took a single step back.

"Add stealthy to that list I was giving you," Cade said, eyes wide and cheeks slightly flushed. "I'm going to have to call you back. Let me know what you think of those files."

"Sorry," she muttered, lifting her free hand hip-high in an embarrassed wave. "I suppose being caught eavesdropping is only slightly less embarrassing than getting into your personal space the way I did earlier."

"Don't worry about it," he said, a strained expression on his brow. "Either thing." He tucked the phone into his back pocket, and Lyndy tried not to envy the device. "I'm glad to see you again. I was beginning to wonder if you'd make a reappearance or secretly order your dinner for delivery to the bedroom window."

"Can I do that?" she asked, tossing a contemplative look over one shoulder.

Cade laughed. "No. Not tonight anyway. Weatherman's predicting rain, and the temperatures are dropping. I went out to check the property. The air's bitter cold." He cast a glance at her stove, then pushed his hands into the front pockets of his jeans. "You've had a big day, so I thought I'd make dinner. We can stay in, take it easy, maybe watch a movie or play cards."

"Well, it's all the same because my bedroom window is ancient and makes a terrible sound when it opens. You would've known what I was up to." She followed his gaze to the baking dish and chicken breasts on her counter. "You're cooking?"

He shrugged. "I'd planned to lure you out of your room with food if you didn't come back on your own."

She laughed and Gus kicked in her arms, reminding her she'd had more than one reason to leave the bedroom. "I got the creeps in there alone, so I had to come out. Plus, this guy wants a bottle." She kissed

Gus's head and stroked his back as she made her way to the kitchen table, then strapped Gus into his seat.

Cade slid the baking dish into her preheated oven and set the timer. "I hope you like chicken parmigiana."

Lyndy shook her head, impressed but not surprised. "Everyone loves chicken parmigiana. I can't believe you cook, too. It doesn't seem fair."

Cade's mouth tipped into a lazy half smile. "What do you mean by *too*? What else do I do?"

She smiled as she tightened the lid on Gus's finished bottle. "You protect damsels and babies in distress for starters."

"True."

"How'd you learn to cook?" Lyndy returned to Gus with the bottle, more eager than she should be for Cade's answer.

"Necessity," he said. "There wasn't always enough money or food to go around when I was young, so I learned to make the ingredients we had last as long as possible for my siblings and me. I had to get creative with the cheap stuff, but I made it into a game, and I wasn't terrible at it. I know because even my older brother, Sawyer, ate without complaints. I still play around with recipes sometimes, but tonight, I went traditional."

Lyndy took in the touching story, the way he stepped in and met a need then and now without being asked, and she warmed impossibly further toward him. Cade Lance was definitely more than a handsome face.

An hour later, Lyndy finished the last bite of the best meal she'd eaten in ages. Her stomach was full and her brain was halfway to a carb coma from the double helpings of angel-hair pasta and parmesan-topped chicken. "That was amazing."

Cade carried their plates to the sink and rinsed them. "Thank you." He loaded the dishwasher and wiped down his work space.

"You don't have to do that," she said, pushing onto her feet to help. "You cooked. You don't have to clean, too." Though she appreciated his willingness. Sam had never done either. His view of the world was a little more black-and-white; or maybe pink-and-blue was the better analogy. She hadn't noticed until they'd bought the farm and moved in together, but Sam had a definite idea about what his roles would be in their relationship and none of those included anything that looked remotely like housework or shopping. And he'd once chastised her for mowing the lawn, even though it was her day off and she'd meant to surprise him.

Cade slung a dish towel over one shoulder and leaned his backside against the counter, successfully blocking her access to the sink. "I made the mess. I clean it up."

She frowned. "That's not how division of labor works."

"Why don't you choose the movie. Maybe Gus can help."

Lyndy narrowed her eyes. "Fine."

"So you'll accept his help?" Cade asked.

Lyndy fought the urge to smile or stick out her tongue.

Cade turned back to the sink with a grin. "No chick flicks."

"Sorry. Gus likes chick flicks." Lyndy collected her baby from the swing, where she'd placed him after his bottle. Gus had enjoyed the soothing motion, music and lights while the grown-ups enjoyed dinner.

To Lyndy's surprise, the conversation had been nearly as good as the food. Cade had been candid and charming. Sharing more than she'd expected and listening intently as she shared in return. They'd talked at length about their jobs, hometowns and futures. She suspected that most of what he'd asked had been by design, intended to unearth details about her life that would be useful to the case at hand. Not really a casual dinner conversation at all. But she didn't mind. Cade had made her feel at ease when she needed it most. And he'd been forthright about his goals and future. Cade wanted to see Fortress Defense grow. He was enthusiastic and single-minded in the endeavor. Everything else would come in second for a long while, and she understood that kind of dedication. It was how she felt about raising Gus to be a good and honorable man. For her, every-

thing and everyone else needed to get in line. Her
goal probably seemed small and silly to Cade, a man
who'd seen the world and started a thriving business
with friends, but to Lyndy, her one goal was everything. And his goal only reminded her that Cade
wasn't in the market for a relationship, and he didn't
have time for a family. Not that he wanted one. He'd
made that crystal clear the night they'd met. He was
afraid he might discover he was like his father. He
didn't want to make some poor woman a guinea pig,
and she didn't want to be one. Though, from what
she'd seen so far, she couldn't imagine he had a selfish or sinister side.

He passed her on his way to the couch, power-
ing on the television while she played with Gus on
the floor. A strange tension seemed to roll off him,
and she knew instinctively where his thoughts had
gone. "Lyndy?"

She pinched her eyes shut, knowing she'd be unable to look his way if he asked once more about
her intentions toward him at the café, then again in
her kitchen.

"We should probably still talk about…"

The phone cut him short.

He shifted on the cushion with a sigh, retrieving
the phone from his pocket. "Cade Lance."

Lyndy dared a look in his direction, gauging the
content of the call and wondering how to apologize
for her earlier behavior without embarrassing herself again.

Cade's expression grew more grim with each passing second. "All right," he said finally, his voice thick and low. "I'll let her know."

Lyndy felt her bones go soft and her stomach coil. "Something happened," she guessed. "Something bad."

Cade worked his jaw a moment, processing or perhaps choosing his words.

"Say it," she demanded. "Tell me."

"There's been another attack."

Chapter Six

Cade carried the bulbous little car seat to his truck with Gus tucked inside. Lyndy had made the task look easier than it was. The contraption was heavy and awkward, and Cade was certain he'd knock it into something and somehow hurt the baby, or at the least make him cry. He would consider either a complete fail, and he never failed.

Lyndy opened the passenger-side door with trembling hands. "Thanks for carrying him."

"It's no problem." And he was secretly thankful for the carrier. He wasn't sure how he would've responded if she'd handed him the baby directly. He'd made it twenty-seven years without holding an infant, and tonight wasn't the night he wanted to learn a new skill.

"Here," Lyndy said, motioning to the open rear door of his extended cab. "The car seat will snap into place on the base."

Cade moved closer. He'd seen her remove the seat when they'd returned from town, but he hadn't paid any attention to how she'd set the thing up on the way there. He rested the little pod on the base, feigning confidence. Nothing happened. He wiggled and shimmied the seat until it slid in his grip, causing Gus to throw his hands wide and wrinkle his pink face. The prelude to a scream. Cade cursed inwardly. "It doesn't fit."

"It fits. You have to turn it around. Gus needs to face backward for a year."

"Why?"

Lyndy stepped against him, guiding his hand to turn the carrier until an audible click sounded and the car seat locked securely into the base. "Because it's the law. There. He's ready."

Cade dropped his hands away, determined to ignore the undeniable heat passing between them, despite the predicted drizzle of icy rain. He supposed part of the problem was a natural physical attraction. To be expected between two young, single people. The rest was likely a result of heightened emotions and increased adrenaline. Not to mention the internal, unspoken need for an outlet. It was the reason there were baby booms about a year after any major tragedy. People turned to one another for comfort. And at the moment, Cade needed to turn away from the woman standing too closely beside him and find another outlet. "Ready?"

The drive to the hospital was long and laced with tension. He'd planned to address the issue of their attraction casually after dinner. Make sure they were on the same page about personal boundaries and professionalism, but the call had put a stop to that, and he couldn't bring himself to mention it now. Not when they had no idea what they would find at the hospital. He doubted the Tom Cat's newest victim would be unconscious and hospitalized if her condition wasn't serious. And he suspected seeing her would be more difficult for Lyndy than she realized.

"You don't have to see her," he said, hoping to ease Lyndy's burden. "The detective said she's unconscious and pretty beat up. Maybe you can just speak with Detective Owens instead."

"I'd like to meet her," Lyndy said. "I feel like I should. It's the least I can do, considering my escape is likely the reason he acted out again so soon. From what I read online, his attacks were usually months in between. I want to let her know I'm here for her, and she's not alone."

Cade parked in the hospital's visitor lot and went around to help Lyndy with Gus. The temperature had dropped since they'd left her home a short while ago, and the rain had turned to snow in the air. Slush on the ground.

She removed Gus from the harness, leaving his seat behind. "Hey, little man," she cooed, cradling him to her chest and swaying gently to an unheard song. "Do you mind handing me that sling?"

Cade passed her the length of material spread across her seat. He'd seen her use it to carry Gus before.

"Thanks." She turned the baby in his direction. "Hold him while I put it on?"

He stepped back. "What?"

"I need to arrange the material. It's easier if I'm not holding him."

Cade stared. Arms glued to his sides. "Maybe I can help you with the material."

Lyndy stepped forward, and Cade stepped back. She cocked her head and narrowed her eyes. "Are you afraid of my baby?"

"No."

"Then take him."

Cade shook his head. "He doesn't know me. I don't want to scare him. Or drop him. Maybe just put him in his seat while you fix the sling."

Determination furrowed her brow, and she turned the baby expertly, arranging him along the length of one forearm. "Bend your arm like mine."

She gripped Cade's wrist and wrenched his arm into position when he didn't comply. "I'm going to move him into your arm, and you're not going to drop him, because that's ridiculous. When was the last time you dropped anything you were holding?"

Cade wanted to say he dropped things every day, all the time, only a few minutes ago, but it wasn't true, and it was too late. She set the baby in his grip, wedged between his arm and chest. The little blue pacifier bobbed in his mouth.

"Hey," Cade said in greeting.

Gus locked eyes with him and cooed. Lyndy had

secured his hat beneath his chin, framing his pudgy face. His mouth opened slightly, lips parting in a wide toothless smile. The pacifier tilted away, and Gus chomped down, setting it back into motion.

"Come on," Lyndy said, already headed for the hospital, her smug expression giving a little kick to his chest.

Cade easily matched his pace to hers, feeling nonsensically proud of the fact Gus hadn't screamed when she'd handed him off. "I thought you wanted to put him in the sling."

"I will, but you're doing such a nice job, and he's happy, so why interrupt?" She grinned mischievously. "Besides, I saw the mild panic on your face when you carried his car seat to the truck."

He smiled back. "Mean."

She bumped playfully against him as they walked. "You're right. Sorry. I can take him whenever you're ready."

Cade glanced at Gus, whose narrow eyebrows moved high on his forehead as he gaped at the brightly lit building ahead and babbled delightedly about the view. White lights had been strung through barren trees and along the rooflines. Holiday well-wishes were painted on the broad atrium windows and doors. "Maybe once we're inside," he said.

Lyndy's pleasant expression fell as they reached the sidewalk outside the Emergency Room, reminding Cade of the gravity of the visit.

"You should know that seeing this victim might

cause a resurgence of the emotions you experienced after your attack," he warned. "Sometimes a simple sound or scent can set it all off again. Seeing her is almost certain to."

"I'm fine," she said. "Do you want me to take Gus now? I think you've proved my point."

"What? That I could carry him across a parking lot without dropping him? Give me a little more time. I'm kind of a klutz."

Lyndy stopped to give Cade a long, slow review. "I doubt that, and no. The point was that I trust you, and so does Gus."

Gus cooed, as if on cue, and something in Cade's tight chest unfurled.

The glass hospital doors parted, and Lyndy reached for her baby. She tucked him fluidly into the ring of fabric around her body and smiled. "Nice work, Lance."

He snorted at the official-sounding clip to her words, thoroughly enjoying the praise. "Thanks."

A moment later, the pungent slap of hospital scents knocked the smile off his lips. The hallmark odors of bleach, stale coffee and bandages met them at the threshold and stripped every nice feeling away. Cade had visited too many brothers in direct care units and military treatment facilities that smelled just like this one, and those friends hadn't come home. He fought against the visceral gut punch, instantly thankful Lyndy had taken her son back.

She stopped at a cart selling flowers and balloons

near the elevators and removed Gus's hat. "Carnations or daisies?" she asked Cade, sincerely, as if he knew what either looked like. Sunflowers or roses, sure, but carnations and daisies?

"The yellow ones."

She bought a small bouquet, then motioned him down the hallway. "They brought me in this way the other night. I'm guessing the paramedics would've done the same with the new victim. Hospital staff won't be permitted to tell us where we can find her. HIPAA," she added in explanation. "But we should at least be able to find a cop who can point us to Detective Owens."

Cade squared his shoulders and matched her determined pace.

Detective Owens soon appeared outside a line of pulled curtains. Lyndy moved confidently in his direction, passing a nurse in the busy space without a glance. The man in scrubs took notice but didn't stop her from breaching the restricted area where Owens spoke with a uniformed officer. She slowed when the lawmen looked up.

The officer's face was pale and drawn. His expression said more than he probably ever would about what he'd seen tonight.

"Oh no," Lyndy whispered, casting a pleading look onto Cade. "Do you think she…didn't make it?"

"I don't know," Cade muttered, knowing firsthand there were worse things for the officer to have seen than death. "I guess we'll find out."

LYNDY WATCHED THE men's expressions as Cade extended a hand to each. "Detective. Officer. Thanks for the call."

Owens bobbed his head, his attention fixed on Lyndy and Gus. "How are you and the little guy holding up?"

"Okay." She kissed her baby's head and said yet another prayer of gratitude for that truth. "Gus is doing better than me, but that'll always be my preference."

"Ain't that the truth," the older man said. "I've got three of my own and seven grandkids now. How about this one?" He smiled at Cade. "How's he working out for you?"

Lyndy felt the heat spreading over her chest, neck and cheeks, as if the three men before her might be able to read her mind, and all the utterly inappropriate things she'd thought about Cade Lance in the last hour alone. "Good," she said, hoping the flush of color to her skin might be misconstrued as anxiety over the situation instead of what it really was. Lust. "How's the woman? Is she still here in the ER or has she been given a room?"

"She's still here," Owens said. "She's stabilized, so she'll be admitted soon. Her family's on their way from out of town. She's a few years younger than you, though another dead ringer. A senior at the local college."

Cade cleared his throat and widened his stance. "What can you tell us about the attack?"

Owens frowned, his remorseful gaze moving to Lyndy briefly before meeting Cade's eyes once more. "She was grabbed from behind. Her mouth covered. The man was taller and stronger. He pulled her against him and whispered Lyndy's name into her ear."

Lyndy's heart froze. "What?" Her lungs burned from the gust of air that whooshed out of her, and her ears began to ring.

The detective shifted uncomfortably. "She told responding officers that he repeated those two words throughout the attack. Your first name and your last. Calm and collected, in slow, level whispers while she screamed for help. No chance of identifying him by voice, and she didn't see his face."

"How's that possible?" Cade asked, while Lyndy willed herself to breathe so she wouldn't faint with Gus in her arms.

The officer's stricken expression darkened and his chin tipped in defiance. "He attacked from behind. It was dark, and after the first blow her vision blurred. Add fear and panic to the mix, and she could barely recall what she'd been doing before he grabbed her. He hit and kicked her to within an inch of her life, then left her under a streetlamp where we'd find her in time. He called it in himself to be sure."

"That's not like him," Cade said, echoing Lyndy's thoughts. Tom had killed his last few victims, and he'd meticulously covered his trails in every case.

The officer dipped his chin in a nearly imperceptible nod. "We think he wanted to send a message."

"To whom?" Lyndy whispered, afraid she already knew.

Owens and the officer exchanged a look, but neither answered.

The tremor that had begun in Lyndy's hands spread through her body. A woman had been beaten, nearly to death, while a monster repeated her name. This was Lyndy's fault. Someone had been punished because Lyndy had gotten away. She forced her sticky, swollen tongue to work and willed herself to be brave. "What's her name?" she whispered, realizing only then that she didn't know.

"Carmen," Detective Owens said. "Carmen Dietz."

"When can I see her?"

The officer's gaze jumped to the curtain at his side. "You should probably give it a few hours or wait until morning. She's not awake, and she'll look better once some of the swelling goes down."

"I don't care how she looks," Lyndy said. "She's here because of me." She turned her attention to Owens. "Do you think there's any chance I met this guy through my work? We don't do job placements in the towns where other attacks have occurred, but I meet a lot of people. I could get you a list of men I've spoken with, interviewed and placed in jobs this year. I'll need to talk to my manager to get a full account, but if I met the lunatic through my work, there will be records."

"We're already looking into that," Detective Owens said, "but it's unlikely you met him through your place of business. The feds' profile suggests he's already gainfully employed, likely in some capacity that allows him to travel."

"But you're still looking at my work ties."

He shrugged. "I'm a strong believer in due diligence. Feds have been wrong before."

Satisfied, Lyndy turned to the curtain where the officer's traitorous glance had darted. Her insides churned. She reminded herself to breathe as her sweaty fingers slid over the waxy paper around her bouquet. "I want to leave these on her nightstand for Carmen."

Cade turned with her, strong and confident at her side. She wasn't alone, and neither was Carmen. Lyndy would be there for her now, and they would get through this together.

She reached for the thin cotton wall, then stepped inside the drawn curtain.

The monster's work came gruesomely into view.

A gasp of air escaped her as she instinctively angled her baby away from the hospital bed. Carmen's grossly swollen and misshapen face barely seemed human. Her eyes were nearly invisible beneath the newly stitched and deeply purple skin. Thick layers of gauze wrapped her head and each arm had been encased in a heavy pink cast. Her lips were split, and IV lines connected her to a mass of machines. The rest of her body was hidden beneath white hospital blankets, but Lyndy could easily imagine what her abdomen and torso looked like. If he'd done all this to her face, a face that had once looked like Lyndy's, the rest would be just as bad. Or worse.

A cascade of hot tears rolled over Lyndy's cheeks, and her breaths grew shuddered. This could have been her.

It could have been Gus.

A pair of strong arms wound around her, turning and pulling her and her baby away from the scene before them. She didn't need to look to know it was Cade, the man who'd become her personal fortress of strength and comfort. She curled her fingers into the fabric of his shirt, crushing the flowers between them.

A small complaint rose from Gus.

"I've got you," Cade whispered, tightening his protective arms and holding her as she cried. He'd been right about the emotions, she realized. A freight train of terror and desperation hit her hard and fast enough to buckle her knees, and all she could do was let it out as quietly as possible for Gus's sake, while Cade supported her through it.

Shockingly, when the tears had dried, Gus was snoring, his head resting peacefully against Cade's chest.

Lyndy wiped her eyes, then slid her fingers between her son and their protector, shifting him back against her alone. "Sorry," she whispered.

"Do you want to sit?" Cade asked, releasing her in the direction of a small wooden armchair.

She didn't have the strength to pretend otherwise, so she lowered herself onto the seat at Carmen's bedside and snuggled Gus against her.

Cade poured a glass of water from the plastic pitcher on the nightstand, then passed it her way. He took the crushed flowers and set them beside the returned pitcher. Lyndy sipped the water to steady her nerves.

The curtain opened and Detective Owens slipped inside. "Well, Carmen's attack has been leaked."

"What?" Lyndy set her cup aside, swapping it for the offered digital tablet in the detective's hand.

"We were first on the scene after his call, and we intentionally kept it under wraps. The paramedics and hospital staff were instructed to do the same. No need to give this guy what he wants."

Lyndy turned her attention to the tablet. A local news article centered the screen. Coverage of a young woman's attack and speculation surrounding the Kentucky Tom Cat Killer.

"He probably alerted the media himself," she said, skimming the article for some detail about Carmen that would provide a connection between them beyond appearance.

Cade moved in close. "The hat," he said, pointing to the screen. "I saw a man in a plain black ball cap like that outside the café a few minutes before the window broke."

Breath caught in Lyndy's throat. "Is it him?" Was it so simple? Tom was so obsessed with the spectacles he caused that he'd accidentally gotten himself on camera?

Detective Owens took the tablet from Lyndy's trembling hand and inspected the image. He nodded several times without speaking, then dug a cell phone from his pocket. "I saw a ball cap like that in the crowd after Lyndy's attack. Let's see if we've interviewed anyone wearing one." Owens pressed the phone to his ear and sidestepped an elderly volunteer carrying a vase of flowers into Carmen's makeshift room. "Excuse me."

The volunteer smiled sweetly at Cade, then Lyndy. Her gaze lingered on Gus's sleeping face a moment, the longing nearly written on her forehead. "Seems like mine were that small yesterday," she whispered, an air of sadness in the words. "They're all grown now, and my grandbabies live too far away to visit, but it's nice I can see so many young families like yours while I'm here. Keep him close," she said. "He'll be ready to leave long before you're ready to let him go."

Fresh emotion clogged Lyndy's throat. She knew the woman was right because she never wanted to let Gus go.

"I'll just leave these here for Ms. Wells and get out of your way." She set the simple glass vase with baby's breath and roses on the stand beside the water pitcher and the smashed bouquet, then turned to leave.

"Who?" Lyndy asked as Cade lifted a hand to stop the older woman.

"Did you say the flowers are for Ms. Wells?" Cade asked, his body rigid and voice tight.

She glanced back at the vase, wrinkles racing across her brow. "Well, yes. Lyndy Wells. Is that not Ms. Wells?" She looked at Carmen for the first time and winced.

"I'm Ms. Wells," Lyndy whispered, thankful to be sitting so she wouldn't collapse. "Who are the flowers from?"

"Owens!" Cade bellowed, already striding toward the nightstand. His skin went pale, then flashed red as he retrieved and read the card.

The flower lady jumped and clutched her necklace as Detective Owens and the officer burst into view, both scowling. Each with a hand on the butt of his sidearm.

Cade pressed the card into Owens's hand, then moved into the old woman's space. "Who bought these flowers?"

"A man in the hallway," she said. "From the flower cart."

"Is he still here?"

"I don't know." Her shoulders climbed to her ears, and her eyes went round with fear.

"What did he look like?" Cade demanded.

"I—I—don't know," she blundered. "He wore brown coveralls, I think. We barely spoke."

Cade burst into a jog with the uniformed officer behind him.

Detective Owens moved to Lyndy's side and handed her the small white card.

A beautiful sacrifice has been made in your name.

Chapter Seven

Cade's military-issue boots gripped the tiled floor as he ran through the crowded emergency room, dodging chairs and people. He scanned the alarmed faces, searching for a man in coveralls as he raced toward the main hallway.

The uniformed officer kept pace behind him, barking orders and acronyms into a walkie-talkie that emitted intermittent responses and white noise. Backup was on the way, but it would be too late. The Tom Cat had made his move. Shown his superiority. And likely made his escape, all before Cade had known he was there.

They skidded to a stop at the first intersection of hallways.

Cade pointed to a kiosk several yards away. "The flowers came from that cart."

The officer jogged away, calling out to the attendant at the register while dozens of people moved in swift determined strides around them. Doctors.

Nurses. Hospital staff and visitors. None of them realizing there was a serial killer in their midst.

Cade bolted back into a run, moving first to the automatic doors for a look at the illuminated lot outside, then at the more dimly lit streets and the low roof above the hospital's main entryway. Nothing but snow and silent cars in the lot. No one on the nearby streets; given the hour and temperature, that was no surprise.

He passed back through the doors at a slower, more methodical pace, willing himself to sense the fiend if he was still near. He retraced his steps through the waiting room and walked the hall, cursing and gripping the back of his neck. *Think*, he told himself, falling back on his military intelligence training. What would someone like Tom Cat do next? The nut had made his point. Had his fun. Now what? Cade had assumed he'd run, but that wasn't right. The Tom Cat was the one calling in news of his escapades. He enjoyed the chaos and fear he'd caused.

Cade turned in a small circle, muscles tightening with instinct. The Tom Cat craved the rush. The adrenaline. He was upping his own game now. And Cade was willing to bet the son of a gun was still here. Watching. Basking in the horror and feeling superior while Cade and the cops chased their tails.

Fear and rage welled in Cade's core as he lengthened his strides, searching every man carefully for signs of that telltale black ball cap. He'd evaluated dozens of people, checked coatracks and men's rooms before another, more nauseating realization hit.

One thing the monster wanted more than acknowledgement without consequences was Lyndy. Cade was charged with protecting her, and he'd left her behind.

His heart in his throat, Cade sprinted back toward the emergency room, praying he hadn't done exactly what the psychopath had wanted.

The halls seemed to lengthen beneath his feet as the realization he might have already failed her twisted knives into his gut. He cut through the waiting room with less grace than before, clipping chairs and winging a nurse who wasn't watching where he was going.

"Lyndy!" he called, unable to wait before yanking back the curtain where he'd left her. "Lyndy!"

His pounding heart seized as the view before him took hold. The space was empty, save for a crumpled, unmade bed, a rumpled bouquet of yellow flowers and the water pitcher on the nightstand.

His ears rang and the world tilted. How could it be? How long had he been gone? Where was Detective Owens?

"Cade?" Lyndy's voice turned him on his heels. She rubbed Gus's back in the sling and looked expectantly at him with those big, trusting eyes.

He inhaled deeply for the first time in too long and his head went light.

A small smile formed slowly on her perfect mouth

as she headed for the nightstand. "They moved Carmen to a room. I forgot her flowers. I guess you didn't find him."

"No." Cade rubbed a heavy hand across his mouth and bit back a fervent round of relieved cursing. He thought he'd lost her, and the pain had been profound. For one moment he'd felt...vulnerable, and the notion left him speechless. Statistically speaking, the Tom Cat was probably some middle-aged nobody stuck in a dead-end job with no friends, money or personality. Cade was a trained marine and hired protector. Tom's havoc shouldn't have been able to reach him emotionally. Not like that. And it had. The reason for it stood before him, gently stroking her son's fuzzy brown hair and clutching a mashed bouquet of flowers.

"You look spent," she said, trading the flowers for the pitcher and filling a cup. "Maybe water will help."

Maybe whiskey will help, he thought, shaking himself off. He took the cup and guzzled it, then reached for Lyndy, determined to keep her close from now on.

He opened the curtain and ushered her toward Detective Owens as he traded words with a pair of uniformed officers.

"Owens ordered an escort," she said. "The officers will follow us home and sit outside the house tonight."

"A protective detail." Cade wholeheartedly approved. Three men guarding Lyndy and Gus were better than one. If the Tom Cat managed to get near her again, all three men had been trained to use a sidearm and hit a moving target if necessary. Two could even make an arrest if the shots didn't kill him.

"Don't take this the wrong way," she whispered, "but you look like I feel, and that's not great."

Before he'd thought better of it, Cade stopped moving and wrapped his arms around her, careful not to disturb Gus.

Lyndy tensed for a moment before melting against him. "I'm okay," she whispered, the words coming thick and tight.

The speaker on the nearby officers' walkie-talkies engaged and a male voice rattled through. "I've got something. Elevators. North hall."

Owens met Cade's gaze above Lyndy's head as the uniforms broke away. He appraised him with sharp eyes and a hefty amount of scrutiny. The embrace was unprofessional. It crossed lines, and Owens would likely never recommend Fortress to anyone again, but Cade couldn't will his arms to release her. Instead, he lowered his mouth to her cheek and whispered. "We've got to go."

She turned stoically away, her arms immediately wrapping the sleeping baby in her sling, her absence leaving Cade's chest hollow and cold.

He stuck to her side as they moved with purpose toward the north hall, following Owens and the uniforms. Cade's senses were on high alert, his every nerve on edge, muscles tensed. Hyperaware of everyone and everything, especially the woman and child beside him.

Soon, the officer who'd gone to speak with the worker at the flower stand came into view outside a bank of elevators. He raised one hand to gain the group's attention. In the other hand was a pair of brown coveralls.

LYNDY LOWERED GUS into his crib with shaking hands. She'd held it together through his bath and bottle, thankful he'd slept through the horrors of the hospital the way only an infant could. He'd likely wake her before she found two moments of sleep for herself, but that was the life of a single mother. She slid the small dial on the baby monitor until the indicator light came to life, then she crept from his room, companion speaker in hand.

She paused outside the door to gather her wits before facing Cade, and attempted to model herself after his strong example, outwardly anyway. Gus deserved at least that much from her, and at the moment, she preferred feigning strength to admitting she was seconds away from booking two one-way tickets to Peru.

"You okay?" Cade asked, drawing her eyes open. He'd asked her the same question countless times since they'd met. A good indicator that she didn't look okay. In other words, she'd have to try harder if she wanted to convince either of them that she was fine.

"I'm doing super," she answered with a wry smile. "You?"

"Oh, you know," he said, matching her overly casual tone. "Not bad. Thinking about some sweet tea."

Her smile widened. "Oh yeah?"

Cade stepped aside and stretched one arm toward the kitchen. "After you."

She peeled herself off the wall and forced a little swing into her hips. If she was going to pretend everything was fine, she might as well go all out. "Any news from Owens or the federal agents?"

"Only that the coveralls recovered from the elevator have been delivered to the lab. Techs will process it for fibers, hairs, residue, anything that might hint at who was wearing them and where they've been outside the hospital. It was a cocky move on the Tom Cat's part, but I suspect he'll only get worse." He retrieved the tea from the refrigerator and filled two mason jars already waiting on the counter.

She accepted the offered jar. "I'm hoping cocky also means easier to catch."

The air in the room seemed to thicken and Cade's jaw locked.

"Or does bolder mean more dangerous?" she guessed, wincing at the image of Carmen that flashed through her mind.

Cade's eyes were dark as he leveled her with his

trademark stare. "Not more dangerous to you. And not to Gus."

"But to other women," Lyndy said, setting the tea aside in favor of wrapping her shaky arms around her middle.

He moved in on her then, eyes locked on hers. The confident swagger in his gait fully derailed her train of thought. "The police and FBI are handling that. You want to tell me how you're really doing? If we're going to be spending so much time together and not sleeping, I think we should at least be honest with each another. Don't you?"

"I'm fine," she said, willing the words to be true.

And if being honest meant having the talk he'd suggested earlier about her attempt to kiss him twice, then no, she didn't think that was best. *Unless he felt the same way*, she thought, far too hopefully.

"Not likely," he answered.

For a moment she wondered if he'd heard her thoughts. Relief flooded her when she realized he'd been talking about her personal assessment of her condition. Which was a definite lie.

Cade raised the jar to his lips, one broad palm curled around the cup as he took a long, deep drink.

She tried not to laugh as she became both thankful and disappointed that she wasn't his cup of tea. *Literally and figuratively.* If he wanted her the way she wanted him, they'd be goners. Too distracted, naked and defenseless to see Tom coming.

"Let me know when you're ready to talk," Cade

said, returning the drained and sweating jar to the countertop.

She mentally reworked her earlier evaluation as she watched him head for her living room with his signature self-assurance. Cade was probably never defenseless. Naked, distracted or otherwise.

He caught her eye from his position on her sofa and watched her silently, with knowing eyes. She was far from fine, and they had a lot to talk about, beginning with her stalker, what he'd done tonight and what could possibly be yet to come.

She moved slowly in his direction, fighting against the rush of awful memories all trying to pull her under. "Tom came to the hospital," she said, kicking off the miserable conversation and sinking onto the sofa beside him. "Do you think he was there to see Carmen, or was he trying to lure me out?" And was it possible he'd followed her home?

She checked for the cruiser outside her front window. The officers were still there, but that didn't mean Tom wasn't. She'd learned tonight that he could be anywhere at any time.

"I don't know," Cade answered her nearly forgotten question. "Owens is reviewing hospital security footage with the feds now, hoping to get a look at someone the right size for the coveralls coming or going. Local uniforms are canvassing the building and nearby businesses. I still can't believe he was in the building and we missed him. He never should've been able to get that close."

"I hate knowing Carmen was hurt because of me, and that Gus might be." Her gut clenched, and a wave of heat crawled up her neck, pooling bile in her mouth. The thought of her baby in the hands of the deranged psychopath who'd beaten Carmen beyond recognition made her stomach churn and her face go numb. She set the tea onto her coffee table, then tipped over, resting her hot cheek against the cool cushion, certain she'd be sick.

The couch shifted beneath her, and Cade walked away. He returned a moment later with a glass of ice water and a wet dishrag. He set the water on the floor where she could reach it, then spread the cool wet cloth over her forehead. "Breathe."

She pulled in a fresh breath and felt her lungs expand. She blew the air out and repeated the process slowly and intentionally until the room stopped spinning and the black dots in her peripheral vision faded away. Then, as if nearly puking in Cade's presence wasn't bad enough, a round of tears began to leak from the corners of her eyes. So much for feigning brave.

Cade presented a handkerchief.

She mopped the renegade drops from her cheeks with a self-deprecating groan. "Thanks. You carry a handkerchief?"

"Yeah." He lowered himself to the floor beside her water. "My granddad gave them to all his grandsons. As far as I know, we all still carry them."

"That's nice," she said. "I've always wanted a big family, but it was just Mama, Grandmama and me."

He scanned her, searching for what, she wasn't sure.

Changing the subject seemed like a good idea. "I'm sorry you were dragged into this," she said, adjusting the cool cloth and feeling slightly less ill. "Talk about drawing the short straw. Your company was probably founded to protect normal people from everyday problems. Frenemies and exes. Maybe a stalker or a disgruntled former employee. Somehow you got stuck between me and a serial killer." A wave of guilt brought the nausea back around. "I'm a disaster magnet."

He snorted. "You think I feel unlucky?"

She raised her brows in challenge. "Aren't you? You're here with me. Is there anyone I haven't put in danger? Gus. You. Every blond-haired, blue-eyed twentysomething female in three counties."

Cade shook his head. "You haven't put me in danger, and I will protect you and Gus. That's a promise."

"Some serial killers are never caught," she said, allowing the panic to swell. "What then?" Even if there wasn't a time limit for his protection, she couldn't go to work while being stalked like this, and if she couldn't work, then her bank account would eventually run dry and her ability to pay him would vanish.

"I won't leave you," he said. "Not until your peace and safety are restored."

Lyndy closed her eyes to stop them from rolling. He probably believed it, but everyone she cared about left eventually.

She swiveled upright on autopilot, caught off guard by the unprompted thought. She didn't care about Cade. Not like that. She was attracted to him, sure, but she'd just met him, and attraction was different than caring. She blamed the intensity of their circumstances for her confusion. She was probably experiencing the opposite version of the Nightingale syndrome, except instead of saving her from a deadly injury or illness, Cade was protecting her from a human killer, and she was getting everything all mixed up in her head.

"I never leave a job unfinished or a client unsatisfied," he continued, tossing her thoughts back to the gutter. A place they'd frequented since his arrival and despite the atrocities around them. Or maybe because of them. Who wouldn't need a distraction at a time like this?

She swallowed at his unfortunate choice of words and tried to pay attention.

"You're stuck looking at my face everywhere you go until the Tom Cat is caught or you send me away."

"I wouldn't send you away," she said softly, and her insides pinched. Maybe it was his promise to leave her satisfied or the look in his eyes as he refocused on her mouth, but she was sure he meant it. And she didn't want Cade to leave. She liked having him around. He was kind and thoughtful and brave.

He let her do what she wanted, then backed her up while she did, like a true partner.

Slowly, his gaze returned to meet hers. "Then I'll stay as long as you want me."

Lyndy let her head fall back until it rested on the cushions and the ceiling came into view. "Okay." What had happened to the sensible, levelheaded woman she used to be? Where was her small, predictable life with intense concerns about calories and daily step counts? And why had any of those things ever seemed so important?

"Do you think Tom intends to hurt more women?" she asked, recalling the awful note attached to his flowers. "He called Carmen a sacrifice in my honor."

"He hurts women because he's insane," Cade said, his voice lowering. "He doesn't do any of this because of you. You're a victim. Not a cause. Or a reason. Keep reminding yourself of that, because he's probably going to keep trying to manipulate you into thinking otherwise."

"Manipulate me?" She lifted her head and locked gazes with him once more. "Into doing what? Giving myself over to him so he'll stop hurting others?"

"Maybe, but killing you won't stop him. A man like this won't stop until he's caught."

Lyndy locked her gaze on his as a wave of resolve rushed through her. "Then let's make sure he's caught."

Chapter Eight

Lyndy woke to the rich, buttery aroma of pancakes and the thick, greasy scent of bacon.

Shafts of sunlight danced above her, angling down from the window to the carpet beyond the couch where she'd apparently fallen asleep. *When did that happen?*

She squinted and rolled onto her side, trying to get her head around the strange situation. She never slept on the couch, and who was cooking if she was still lying there?

Gus laughed, and Lyndy's heart leaped.

She swung herself into a seated position and stared wide-eyed at the scene before her, unsure if she was really awake.

Gus was strapped into his highchair and belting bold, boisterous belly laughs as Cade flipped pancakes in a skillet.

Lyndy was on her feet in the next heartbeat, recalling every event that had brought her here in vivid detail. She drifted in the direction of her son, buoyed by the sound of his laughter and so thankful to Cade for the extra rest and breakfast—not to mention the joy he was giving her baby—that she was sure to burst.

"Morning," Cade said, taking notice and looking somewhat guilty as she entered the room.

She unfastened Gus's safety strap and lifted him for a cuddle.

Cade ferried the platter of pancakes to the table and set them beside a plate piled high with bacon, then pulled out a chair. "I hope you're hungry. I'm usually flipping hotcakes for four hungry men. I think I went a little overboard on the batter."

"And the bacon," she said, snagging a piece with her free hand and taking an immediate bite. "An error in my favor." Her eyes fluttered shut in pleasure. "I haven't had bacon since Gus was born. I was hooked on it during my pregnancy and gained more than forty pounds. I'm still trying to work it off."

Cade's mischievous grin heated her cheeks. Thankfully, he shook his head and kept whatever he'd been thinking to himself.

She took a seat and arranged Gus on her lap, then showered him in kisses. "How are you, my sweet little man?" she asked, nuzzling his neck and making him coo. "Mama feels rested. I'd almost forgotten what this felt like, but I love it."

Cade set a cup of coffee in front of her, then delivered a plate and set of silverware. The syrup and butter came next. "Anything else you need?"

"Just a little company," she said, pointing to the chair across from her.

Cade obeyed, then filled a plate with food and dug in. "I wasn't sure if I was overstepping. Taking the baby from his room when he woke, feeding him, helping myself to your groceries again. No offense intended."

Lyndy rolled her eyes. "None taken. I haven't slept this long in over a year." Not since Sam had died. "And I don't think anyone, other than my mother, has ever made me breakfast."

Cade stopped chewing and stared. "No one?"

"Nope." She forked a pair of golden pancakes from the stack and centered them on her plate.

"Sam didn't cook for you?" he asked, genuine curiosity creeping into his tone.

"Sam didn't cook," she said flatly. In hindsight, Sam hadn't done a lot of things, but the inequality in their relationship had never seemed so significant before. "He was...traditional."

Cade wrinkled his nose. "A misogynist?"

"No," she laughed. "Not like that. He was never mean about it."

Cade pursed his lips and tented his brows. "Well, I like to cook, and I love pancakes. So anytime you're in the mood, just holler."

"I will," she said, wondering if the smile on her face was permanent. She hadn't stopped grinning since the moment she'd woken. "You're going to make some woman very lucky one day. Or some man. No judgment."

Cade set his fork aside with a laugh, then lifted his coffee. "I don't think so. I'm sure no man could handle me, and fairly confident no woman would put up with me. I'm not all bacon and pancakes."

Lyndy smiled, wanting more information, but not sure it was okay to ask. "Fair enough."

"What about you?" He examined her with sharp, probing eyes. "You'd planned to get married. You had a terrible loss. Then a baby. But it's been a year. Why aren't you dating now?"

She shrugged. "I guess I was busy grieving at first. Then I was trying to figure out how to have a healthy pregnancy, then how to juggle work and a newborn. Now I hate the thought of bringing anyone into Gus's life who he might get attached to and miss, in case they leave. That just doesn't seem fair, and I know firsthand that people leave, even if they don't want to. Life happens." And death.

"Right. Can't get your heart broken again if you don't date."

"It's more than that." She shifted uncomfortably, hating the way he'd oversimplified her complicated life. "I've had enough heartbreak to go around, and I'm not interested in inviting more."

Sure, maybe the next guy would live, but what if he didn't? Was that a crazy thing to worry about? Lyndy was a worrier by nature, but she'd never worried about Sam being hit by a sleeping trucker or about herself being nearly abducted by a serial killer, and those much more far-fetched things had happened. So, anything could. She rubbed heavy palms over the chilled skin on her arms, hugging Gus closer and willing her suddenly twisting stomach to settle.

"Fair enough," Cade answered, clearly still satisfied with his black-and-white interpretation of her behavior.

"What about you?" Lyndy asked. "Why wouldn't any woman put up with you?"

He caught her eye and frowned, stretching long legs under the table and leaning back in his chair. "I told you, my old man was a son of a gun. A drinker. Jealous. Mean. And I already look like him. I'm not in any hurry to find out if I'll act like him if the situation's right."

"Fear of failure," she assessed as quickly and flippantly as he'd passed judgment on her. "Got it." She kissed Gus again and nibbled on another piece of bacon.

"No." Cade narrowed his eyes and straightened in his seat. "I just can't be sure I'd do the job justice."

"Who can?" she asked. "And how could we? I spent my entire pregnancy worried about whether or not I could be a good mother to Gus. I had no experience for this job and no partner to share the weight. But in the end, I loved him so much, even before I'd met him, that I was willing to do whatever it took, and I have. That's love. That's relationships in a nutshell. We have to be willing to give the other person all of ourselves and trust them to do the same. It's a little more one-sided for Gus and me, but it's the same concept. If I do all I can to meet his needs and fill his heart, then however much that is, it will be enough."

Cade didn't respond. His gaze moved from her face to Gus's and back.

"You say you don't think you can be a good partner," Lyndy continued, unsure why the subject mattered so much to her, or at all, but determined to say her piece. "You're already a partner. You have been for years. All that time you were in the military. Now with your teammates at Fortress. You guys rely on one another, sometimes for your lives, and you trust each other. That's all it takes. Trust. Loyalty. Dedication and perseverance."

"Is that all?" he asked, a coy smile replacing the cranky frown.

"Sure." Lyndy made a mental note that mind-bending sex probably helped, but she wasn't about to add that at the breakfast table. And to be honest, she'd never had the mind-bending sort, but she wouldn't turn away an opportunity. "We should probably talk about what's on the agenda today."

Cade nodded but averted his eyes.

For a moment, she wondered if he'd had a similar thought about the sex, but she shoved the idea quickly aside. The last thing she wanted to think about was Cade having great sex with another woman when the only sex Lyndy had wanted in a year was with him.

"What do you want to do?" he asked.

Lyndy buried her face in Gus's baby curls and inhaled deeply to ground herself back in the moment. Prepared for an argument, she suggested, "I thought we could go back into town."

Cade froze. "Why would we do that?"

"I told you last night. We have to help the police identify the Tom Cat. I think I fell asleep while I was making a list of all the places I go on a semi-regular basis, but it's a small town. I can make a new list. We've already visited my usual stops, but there are plenty of places I can be expected like clockwork, just not as often. We still haven't visited my office, and I haven't been to the gym in a year, but I was a regular before. Since we don't know how long I've been followed, it's possible I ran into the killer before I quit going. Some of the other victims were fitness enthusiasts."

"But they weren't all from the same town," he pointed out. "They wouldn't have gone to your gym."

"But," she countered, "anyone can buy a day pass. Tom could have first taken notice of them here, then stalked them in their hometowns. We should start at my gym, then move on to the library, grocery and park. I'd like to save my office for last since it seems least likely I met him there, and I'm in no hurry to explain any of this to my coworkers who surely know more than me by now, between the local news and gossip mills."

Cade worked his jaw but didn't protest.

Lyndy interpreted his silence as acceptance, then helped herself to another slice of bacon.

CADE UNDERSTOOD LYNDY'S need to do something, her desire to be useful and even her misplaced sense of responsibility for what had happened to Carmen, but he didn't like any of it. And if it had been his place to tell her as much, they'd still be at her house, where he could better protect her. As it was, he could only offer her instinct and training. There were no protective perimeter options when she was on the move.

The officers who'd kept watch through the night had pulled out just after breakfast. According to Owens, another cruiser would be back at sundown, but Cade was on his own during the day. The Tom Cat's note sent to the hospital had created an all-hands-on-deck situation for the FBI and local PD. Everyone was in agreement. He would act again. The question was only when. And Lyndy wanted to go marching around downtown.

Cade rounded the truck's hood to her side and waited as she removed Gus from his car seat and arranged him in her sling. It was strange to hear her admit she'd been afraid of being a terrible mother when she was so clearly a natural with him. She seemed more in tune with her baby than any mother he'd ever known. Maybe that was because it had just been the two of them for so long, or maybe that was just Lyndy. Maybe she was naturally in tune with everyone. She certainly saw through Cade's masks and pretenses without any trouble. He could only hope she wasn't a mind reader, or he was sure to soon be slapped.

She shut the passenger door and turned to face him, a mix of hope and trust in her eyes. "We can do this," she said. "All we need is some tiny thread to start the whole ball rolling toward finding this guy's identity. The police will get their man, and the female population of Kentucky will be safe once more."

"No problem," he deadpanned, eliciting a smile from Lyndy.

Her cheeks were rosy from the cold, and she'd tugged a knitted pink cap over her hair and ears; a giant round pom-pom sat on top.

"Love the hat," he said, giving the ball a little flick.

"Hey. I made this hat," she said. "Do you want one?"

"Please, no."

She grinned, and he took her hand, feeling much too light for the quest she was on.

"Remember the rules," he warned. "Stay in my sight at all times. And if I say we're done, we're done. You're going to have to trust my survival instincts, since apparently you don't have any."

"Funny," she said, not looking as if she thought he was funny at all. She turned her soft hand beneath his then spread her fingers so he could slide his in between.

He rolled his shoulders and resisted the urge to adjust his jeans. "Whatever you want."

"If only real boyfriends were so accommodating."

Cade flashed his wickedest smile and gave Lyndy's fingers a little squeeze. She had no idea how accommodating he could be.

She stopped at the crosswalk, a crimson blush spilling across her cheeks, and it was all he could do not to grab her and kiss her.

They crossed the street at the signal and headed toward the local gym, a wide one-story building with broad windows and tinted glass doors. He opened one to let her pass inside.

"I haven't been here since my second trimester," she said, taking a long look around the foyer. "My membership ran out the same month Gus was born, so I decided to walk at the park instead. That way I could keep him with me. Clearly not my brightest idea."

Cade frowned as Lyndy's presence turned a number of heads, mostly male. He nodded at the men who stared a moment or two longer than necessary, letting them know she was spoken for. *Exactly like a Neanderthal*, he thought, unimpressed with whatever had gotten into him. Lyndy wasn't territory to be marked, but the idea someone wanted to hurt her, maybe even one of these ogling men, made him want to tell the world that anyone who tried would have hell to pay.

"Morning people," Lyndy said with mock disgust. "Mornings are always packed. I'm sorry, but I'm wired to stay in bed as long as possible."

She was right about it being busy. There was a body on nearly every machine and a respectable mix of ages and fitness levels from what he could see. A near fifty-fifty split between genders. He turned for a better evaluation of the space across from them. Several women on cardio equipment smiled in his direction.

"Do you get stared at like this everywhere you go?" Lyndy asked.

"Usually," he admitted. "I've been told I put people on edge."

She laughed, and he smiled.

"Good morning!" a pert voice interrupted. A young brunette beamed from behind the counter. She wore a logoed shirt and nearly fizzed with a level of enthusiasm Cade couldn't imagine. Her name tag said Becky. "Can I help you with anything?"

Lyndy released Cade's hand and stepped forward, resting her elbows on the tall counter. "Hi, yes. I was a member here about a year ago, but—" she pointed at Gus, gnawing toothlessly on a Santa-shaped teether and drooling like a faucet "—I had a baby, and it's been fun, but I'd love my old body back."

"I completely understand," Becky chirped. "And we can help. A lot has changed here. How about I show you around?"

Cade and Lyndy followed Becky through the members-only turnstile.

She led them room to room, pointing out every obvious thing imaginable.

"This is the men's locker room. This is the ladies'

locker room. This is where we hold spin classes. This is the café."

Lyndy nodded along, oohing and aahing at their guide's ridiculous tour.

Cade focused on the patrons' faces as they turned to watch Becky's little parade.

"This is the sauna," Captain Obvious continued.

Lyndy looked over her shoulder, then twisted at the waist for a better view of the patrons.

Cade slid his arm around her back and tugged her against his side. "Something wrong?"

She looked around again. "I don't think so."

He followed her lead, examining everyone and everything more carefully, but finding nothing and no one of interest.

"We ask that you sign up for treadmills and elliptical machines when we're busy," Becky said, pointing to a row of clipboards hanging on the wall beside the cardio machines. It was the first piece of useful information she'd managed, if they were really thinking of joining the gym. "And try to limit yourself to thirty minutes when the wait list is more than three people long. Oh, will you excuse me for a minute?" She hurried toward the desk, where a pair of women in spandex waited.

Lyndy turned a longing look toward the ellipticals, arranged before the window overlooking the street. "I used to love these. I came at night, when I knew the place would be empty, just so I could stay on as long as I wanted. Most nights I did ninety minutes with my favorite audiobook, a view of the town and a smoothie reward."

Cade moved behind her, aligning his chest to her back, and groaned inwardly when he felt her relax against him. The curve of her boldly placed bottom tested his control. He wrapped an arm around her on instinct, splaying his fingers over the gentle curve of her hip. He lowered his lips to her cheek, letting the stubble on his chin graze her ear on the way down. He grinned as he watched her lips part in the reflection of the large window before them.

"You're playing your part in this very well," she whispered. "You seem invested."

"I am, and you make it easy," he said. Though, in truth, she was making things very hard for him, and if she moved another inch to the left, she'd know.

He scanned the street for onlookers but found none of interest. An elderly couple, a crowd of teens laughing loudly. Families. Little Leaguers. Women with strollers. A man and his dog.

A large delivery truck pulled away, and a squat yellow-and-white building came into view across the street. The sign on top proclaimed its name: Sunshine Smoothie. The shop had floor-to-ceiling windows, a long line at the counter and café seating outside. "Is that where you went for your smoothie fix after a workout?"

"Every time."

Sunshine Smoothie would have been the perfect

place to watch Lyndy on an elliptical at night, ninety contented minutes at a time, without her ever knowing.

Cade lowered his mouth to her cheek once more and pressed a testing kiss. "Let's see if he's still watching."

She shivered, then raised her arm, hooking a hand behind his head and pulling him down to her. She let her head fall back and roll to one side, exposing the creamy skin of her neck in offering.

Cade didn't need to be asked twice. He pressed his lips against the tender hollow at the base of her jaw, just below her ear, and inhaled the sweet vanilla and honey scent of her.

Lyndy gave a soft purr of pleasure.

The repetitive blasts of a car alarm sounded outside, and Cade snapped upright, instinct clutching his gut.

He grabbed her wrist and pulled her with him as he raced through the door and onto the sidewalk.

As expected, the lights on Cade's truck flashed, and the horn bellowed.

They crossed the street to find a large rock smashed against the now concave windshield, covered in a spiderweb of cracks. Below the rock, another note rippled on a half sheet of paper in the wind.

Peekaboo. I see you.

Chapter Nine

Hours later, Cade and Lyndy were still in town, a trip he hadn't wanted to make, to begin with. Now his truck was vandalized, another deranged note had been delivered and Cade was hungry. Not a winning trifecta. In fact, he'd had drill sergeants in better moods than his unapologetically nasty one. Which Lyndy had already pointed out twice.

"Try this," she said, passing a tall disposable cup covered in cartoon suns his way.

The air inside Sunshine Smoothie was fragrant with the sweet scents of blended fruit and churned by a blender that never seemed to rest. The interior was perky in the extreme, brightly colored with murals of dancing produce and the sort of music he'd expect at Disneyland. He ground his teeth in annoyance as a pair of FBI agents explained to Detective Owens that there were no witnesses, yet again.

Lyndy wiggled the smoothie. "Trust me. One sip." The cup had a clear lid and a big yellow straw. "Tasty

Tropic was always my favorite. It has bananas, or-
ange juice, coconut and pineapple."

Cade accepted the offering, reminding himself
that his mood wasn't her fault. Though he had no
idea why she wasn't the one ready to go door-to-
door, through the whole darn town, shaking every
man by his neck until one confessed.

She removed Gus from the sling and turned him
to face Cade. She hooked an arm across Gus's chest
and he kicked chubby, dimpled legs. He'd finished
the bottle she'd brought in her bag and decided it was
playtime, obviously thrilled to be rid of the stifling
snowsuit. She hovered him over the tabletop, where
he performed a half-bounce, half-dance routine while
making a fountain of spit bubbles.

Cade fought the unbidden smile twisting his lips.
He needed to hold on to his mood for when he got his
hands on the nut threatening Lyndy and her child.
He pushed the big yellow straw between his lips and
took a gentle pull, hoping whatever was in the cup
would be predictably terrible and restore his ugly
mood. Cade wasn't a fruit guy. Meat, vegetables,
pizza, tacos, yes. Maybe the occasional apple. But
multiple fruits blended with yogurt in a cartoon-sun-
covered cup where smiling suns wore dark glasses,
and an obnoxious script wished him a "Happy Sun-
shiny Day"? *No.*

Lyndy's brows rose in anticipation as the mixture
met his tongue.

Dammit.

It was good. And Cade took a longer, deeper pull, enjoying the smoothie far more than he wanted.

Detective Owens broke away from the agents and ambled in Lyndy's direction. He made a few goofy faces at Gus before turning a more serious look on Lyndy. "I'm sorry you're going through this, Ms. Wells, but I want you to know we're doing everything we can."

She smiled warmly in return. "I believe you are, and it's appreciated."

"What'd you learn?" Cade asked, his smoothie nearly gone.

Detective Owens gave a small shake of his head. "No one saw anything."

"That seems to be a real pattern in this town."

"It's a real pattern everywhere," Owens said. "Most folks have to concentrate just to keep putting one foot in front of the other. Life's busy and demanding, especially this time of year. Christmas is only three weeks away, you know. Besides that, we're preoccupied as a culture and rarely look at strangers longer than necessary. We learn in elementary school that it's rude."

"What about security feeds?"

"So far we've got plenty of footage but no decent angles. We've got the rear of your truck in one, a side shot in another where the hood is out of sight. A great view of the windshield from a rotating camera that caught before and after footage with no in between. There's a camera on the roof of this building, so we might have something there once the manager comes in." Detective Owens checked his watch. "We gave him a call about an hour ago."

Cade felt his blood pressure rise. "What's taking so long? What's more important than catching a serial killer?"

"Nothing!" a new voice called from behind the counter.

A man in a white polo shirt and khaki pants hurried in their direction. "I'm sorry to keep you waiting." He was in his late thirties, with glasses and a sling on one arm. "It's been a harried morning, and no matter how many times I work through my routines with this thing, I never seem to get any faster." He flapped his bent arm like a wing, in case someone hadn't noticed the injury.

Cade didn't like him. He didn't particularly like any man at the moment, but he was sure this one ticked him off. "What happened to your arm?"

"Torn rotator cuff," the man answered congenially. "The result of my courageous battle on the racquetball court."

Cade pushed onto his feet. "When?"

"Uhm." The man straightened, casting a worried gaze from Cade to Lyndy, then Detective Owens. "About six weeks ago now, I guess. Why?"

Cade looked to the cashier, watching raptly from behind the register. "That sound right to you?"

She looked at her manager, then nodded quickly. "I guess so."

Cade returned to his drink. If that guy had been in a sling for six weeks, he wasn't the man who'd attacked Lyndy at the park a few days ago.

"I'm Terri Fray," the man said, extending his good hand to Detective Owens first, then Lyndy. He put the hand in his pocket instead of offering it to Cade. "I manage this store. I got your call while I was at physical therapy. I had to run home and dress for work before coming in. I showered, too—you'd thank me if you knew." He gave a little smile. No one laughed. "Anyway, I didn't know it was an emergency. I was only told there was an act of vandalism on the street, and the police wanted to speak with me at the shop."

"It was my truck," Cade said. "It's in the lot at the end of the block. They're replacing my windshield now."

"Oh." Terri frowned. "What can I do about that?"

Detective Owens stepped forward. "Nothing, but I'd like a look at your security feed. The camera on your roof points in the right direction, more or less, and we're reviewing material from every camera on this block."

Terri cringed. He tipped his head and guided Owens away from the bulk of blatantly eavesdropping customers seated quietly at nearby tables. Cade and Lyndy followed.

"It's a dummy," Terri said. "The equipment is expensive and upkeep is worse, so I just let it go a few years ago. No one steals smoothies and there are very few robberies in town, so I thought it would be okay. I left the camera up as a deterrent in case I was wrong."

Cade rubbed a palm against his forehead.

Lyndy passed Gus to him, and he accepted the child on instinct.

"Hey." Cade's protest came too late. His hands were already around Gus's middle, and pulling him to his chest. They both looked at Lyndy. "What are you doing?"

"Going to the ladies' room. We left home hours ago, and I'm on my second smoothie."

Cade gave the door at the end of the short hall a long look, then led the way with Gus. He knocked, then pressed his way inside and scanned the small area. "All clear."

Lyndy rolled her eyes. "Was there any chance the Kentucky Tom Cat Killer was hiding in the ladies' room?"

"Sounds like I'm not the only one getting cranky," he whispered to Gus on his way out.

"I can hear you," Lyndy called through the closed door behind them.

Cade grinned. "Looks like you won't be getting away with anything when you get older, little man." He tucked Gus against his hip and smiled. Cade dropped an unplanned kiss on the top of the baby's head and realized how thankful he was that he'd been the one answering Fortress Defense's phone when Detective Owens called.

LYNDY TOOK HER time in the ladies' room. She needed to pull herself together before her inner emotional breakdown began to show. She'd been calm, collected and pleasant far longer than she'd thought possible, and despite two delicious smoothies, she wanted to cry. No. She wanted to wail and kick and beat her fists against something, preferably the lunatic wreaking havoc on her life. It wasn't fair that Gus was in danger. That Carmen had been hurt. That one man was outsmarting a team of local police and trained FBI agents. The entire situation was just wrong. And she was about two heartbeats away from curling into a ball and losing it.

She splashed cool water on her overheated face and growled at the pink-cheeked reflection staring back at her. She closed her eyes against the suddenly tear-blurred vision, then pressed the heels of her hands against the lids. "Come on, Wells," she whispered. "Toughen up. All you've got to do is outlast Tom. Keep going until he gets caught."

Several minutes later, she opened the bathroom door and stepped out, half expecting Cade to be waiting on the other side. Instead, he'd moved to the window overlooking the street and seemed to be having a serious conversation with Gus.

Her baby looked incredibly tiny in his arms. Arms she knew would fight to protect him. If she and Gus had to be wrapped up in this nightmare, at least they had Cade. It was too bad he had to leave when it was over. Nonsensical or not, it would hurt to see him go.

"Hello." Terri moved carefully in her direction, his good hand up in surrender. "Sorry. I didn't want to alarm you."

She paused and worked up a smile. "Hi."

"You probably don't remember me," he said, "but I think I remember you. It's been a while, and you didn't have a baby then, but I think you used to stop in at night?"

"I did." Her smile widened. "I don't think we ever met."

"No. I rarely work the counter, but I'm good with faces. Not as much with names."

"Lyndy," she said.

"Right." He bobbed his head in agreement. "I'm sad to say I've seen you on the news. It's awful, isn't it?"

Lyndy did her best not to scream any number of sarcastic remarks. She settled on, "Yes. It is," keeping things short and sweet, but the venom in her voice said what she wouldn't. Terri was an idiot.

His smile drooped. "Well, if you or your boyfriend want another smoothie, they're on the house. I've already told the cashier to provide anything you'd like. Free of charge today."

Lyndy forced a tight smile as she stepped around him and headed for Cade.

He turned to face her and frowned as Terri scurried away. "Owens says we can go. My window's fixed, and the cops have done all they can for now."

"Thank the stars." Lyndy took Gus and kissed his ruddy cheek, more than ready to go home.

Owens lifted a finger, indicating they should wait. He had a phone pressed to his ear and a look of frustration on his face. He turned tired eyes to Cade, grunted, then disconnected the call. "We got something on a private feed. Some kid in an apartment down the street set it up to watch women coming and going from the gym." He shook his head. "That camera caught a man throwing the stone at your truck. He had his back to the camera, but he's wearing a black ball cap like the one you noted outside the café."

Cade stiffened at Lyndy's side, tension rolling off him in waves. "Anything else?"

"Afraid not."

"Approximate height, weight, build, hair color, visible tattoos?"

Owens shook his head again. "There's a good six feet of shadows along the base of the building beside that parking lot at this time of day. Shielded the guy almost completely."

"Thank you," Lyndy said, grabbing her things and shouldering the diaper bag. "Keep in touch."

"Yeah."

Cade opened the door for her, then followed her onto the sidewalk in silence.

She could sense the anger in his strides.

He beeped his door locks open as they approached his truck, and she reached for the door. "What was that guy talking to you about in the hallway back there?"

"The manager?" she asked, strapping Gus into his five-point harness with shaky hands. "Nothing much. He thought he recognized me from my many trips to the shop last year." *And the news*, she thought with a twist to her gut. "He said my boyfriend and I could have free smoothies, but I think that offer ran out once we left."

"Bummer," Cade said, closing the door behind her when she climbed in.

They rode away from town in silence, both clearly lost in thought. Likely about the same thing. Somehow Tom was always near but unnoticed. And even when he made his presence known, he was little more than vapor. Intangible, then gone.

Desperate for a silver lining, Lyndy focused on something nice about the day. "I knew you'd like the smoothie," she said, watching Cade for his reaction. "Now you see why I went there every night."

Cade's jaw tightened as he signaled at the next intersection.

"What?"

"I think that shop is the key to this. The location is perfect for watching you at the gym. Your favorite cardio machines are lined up in front of a window. Your routine was predictable, and the smoothie shop does enough business for the guy to go unnoticed. The setup can't get much better for someone like him. And every night that you bought a smoothie, he got an up close look at his favorite fantasy in the flesh."

"I didn't buy a smoothie every night," she said, a long-faded memory pushing its way to the surface of her tired mind. "Cade. Sometimes my orders were already paid for."

He jerked his face in her direction, eyes narrowed and expression tight. "What?"

"Only once or twice," she said, hurrying to get the words out and half-afraid she'd choke on them. "Sometimes the girl behind the counter wouldn't charge me. She'd say it was on the house. My usual was already made, and someone else had it covered."

"Who?" Cade barked, slowing his truck as he stared at her.

"I don't know."

"Who was the girl behind the counter?"

"I don't know," Lyndy repeated, her shoulders creeping toward her ears. "A teen? Black curly hair. Glasses. I think. I'm not sure. It's been so long. And it wasn't a big deal."

Cade muttered a curse under his breath and wheeled the big truck into a U-turn, causing traffic to weave and horns to blow. "I'd say that's one hell of a big deal."

Chapter Ten

Cade pulled his truck onto the curb outside the Sunshine Smoothie and flung the door wide as Lyndy scrambled down from the passenger seat. He collected Gus and grabbed Lyndy by the hand, then swung the glass door open with unnecessary oomph. Adrenaline spiked and pounded in his veins as he marched through the smattering of patron-filled tables. Finally, their search for a link to the Tom Cat was getting somewhere.

"I don't see Owens," Lyndy said, stating Cade's thoughts aloud. "No officers, either. Did they leave? Did you notice their cars outside?"

"No," Cade admitted, releasing her hand as he pushed his way to the front of the line. "Maybe they're in the back or in Terri's office."

A man in hipster glasses and a bowling shirt scoffed as Cade blew past. "Excuse you!"

Cade glared in the man's direction before pressing his free palm to the counter. "Hey," he called to the teen working the register.

The girl jumped, looking inexplicably guilty and as if she might run. It was her lucky day, because whatever the girl had gotten into, Cade doubted it had anything to do with him. He just needed information. "We were just in here. Do you remember?"

"Yeah."

"We need to talk to the policemen who were with us, or your manager."

The girl shook her head. "You can't. They left. First the cops, then Mr. Fray."

Cade ground his teeth.

"It's okay," Lyndy said, tugging Cade's coat sleeve. "We'll call Detective Owens."

"Hang on," he said, shooting the hipster another look. "You ever work nights?" Cade asked the worker.

"N-no," the little blonde spluttered, her cheeks growing impossibly darker.

"How long have you worked here?"

"S-six months. Why?"

Cade knocked on the counter in frustration. That wasn't long enough, but it was a small town, and this lead was all he had. "You live around here? Maybe you know the girl who worked nights last year?"

"What's her name?"

Cade shot Lyndy a pointed look.

"She had black curly hair and glasses," Lyndy said. "I can't remember her name. We hoped you might."

The cashier's mouth opened. Then shut. A measure of relief crossed her brow, though her skin remained unnaturally pale. She was definitely guilty of something. "Maybe you mean Ramona?" she asked.

"Maybe," Cade said. "How can we get ahold of her to ask? Do you have her contact information? An address or phone number?"

"No."

Cade scowled. "You have to have access to employee contact information."

"Yeah, right." The girl laughed. "Even if I had access to that information, I'm not giving it to you."

Cade pressed his lips against a tirade. Was the world conspiring against him? What was wrong with this day? "Fine. Get me your manager's number. I'll get Ramona's information from him."

Her eyebrows rose in disbelief and defiance. "No."

The overwhelming scent of crushed fruit and yogurt wound into his nose and deepened his frown.

Lyndy inched forward. "Hi," she told the cashier, rewinding the conversations, then turning to the restless crowd behind them, all of whom had settled in to listen instead of complain, even the hipster. "I'm very sorry to have bothered y'all, but this is truly important. We need to find Ramona, so if anyone knows how we can do that, it would be greatly and sincerely appreciated."

The cashier dragged her gaze from Cade's steaming expression to Lyndy's much calmer one. "Ramona hasn't worked here in months."

"Do you know where she works now?" Lyndy asked.

"No."

Cade followed Lyndy's lead and addressed the crowd this time. "How about you guys? Any of you know where Ramona works now?"

"Is Ramona in trouble?" a middle-aged woman wondered.

"No, ma'am," Lyndy replied. "But I think she might be able to help me identify the man who attacked me."

The hipster raised a brow at Cade. "That's what all this is about? Someone attacked your girl, and you're looking for him?"

Cade dipped his chin. The statement was true enough, though Lyndy wasn't really his girl. But the act felt far more authentic than it should in a short period of time.

Satisfied, the hipster removed a cell phone from his jacket pocket and swiped the screen. "I think she lives in the off-campus housing near my sister. I can call and ask."

"Miss?" The middle-aged woman stepped out of line and skirted around the crowd, careful to give Cade a wide berth. "I saw Ramona this morning."

Cade and Lyndy moved away from the counter, and the line reformed.

"Where?" Lyndy asked kindly, a hint of desperation in her voice.

The woman swung an arm toward the big window, pointer finger outstretched. "The diner on the corner. She was waiting tables."

Cade followed her gaze to a small restaurant across the street, separated from the gym by a narrow alley partially blocked by a dumpster. "Thank you." He pulled his phone from one pocket and dialed Detective Owens. The police needed to interview Ramona. He and Lyndy could speak with her now, if they got lucky and caught her at work, but federal agents assigned to the Tom Cat case would want to add her to the possible witness list and get her interview on record. Maybe something she remembered would be the key to naming this psycho.

Lyndy looked visibly shaken as Cade dialed Detective Owens and waited for the call to connect.

He set Gus's carrier on the nearest table and faced him, angling his back to the bulk of the crowd. "You okay?"

She nodded quickly, sipping and releasing air in little puffs. "No." Her eyes darted to the restroom sign on the wall beside them. "I just need a minute."

"I'll be right here," he assured her as the detective answered.

He relayed the new information to Owens while admiring Gus's ability to sleep ten times a day and through absolutely anything. He pinched the cell between his shoulder and ear as he turned for a look down the hallway toward the ladies' room. Instinct clawed at his chest.

"I'll call you back," he told Owens, then stuffed the phone into his back pocket.

He hefted Gus's carrier off the table and went to knock on the restroom door. "Lyndy? Everything okay?"

The door opened easily under pressure of his touch, but the room was dark and empty.

Adrenaline spiked in his veins as he turned for a look into the dining area where he'd just been. He couldn't have missed her on his way there. She hadn't returned to him, but it looked as if she hadn't arrived in the ladies room, either.

"Lyndy?" he called, pushing his voice out and willing her to respond.

He marched through the door marked Employees Only and checked the lounge, supply closets and office. "Lyndy!"

The wobble of a swinging door drew his attention as Gus began to cry. The cashier stared at him, mouth agape. "What are you doing? You're not allowed back here!"

"Lyndy's gone." The words stung on his tongue. He needed to call Owens. Needed to find her. The back door came into view as he paced. "Call the police," he demanded. "Tell them Lyndy Wells was just abducted from your shop. Do it now!"

Cade bolted through the back door and into an alleyway with cars parked along one side. His stomach rolled and his nerves screamed along with her son, wailing in his car seat. If her stalker had been in the alley with a car, she could be halfway to the county border by now. All while he'd been on the telephone!

He moved toward the main road, where he'd left his truck.

Shoppers moved jauntily in every direction, heavily laden with packages and steaming logoed cups. Their voices merry and faces bright. All while Cade's world crashed down around him.

The traffic light changed, halting the stream of cars. The digital screens on each corner seemed to be counting down to another tragedy. One Cade couldn't bear. "Lyndy!"

Gus screamed louder, and a woman with a double stroller and toddling child approached him. Her gaze rolled protectively over Gus, then up to Cade's face. "Are you okay?" She asked, glancing quickly back to the wailing child.

"I'm looking for a woman," he said quickly. "She's small and blonde. Short hair. Blue eyes. She's been taken." His eyes raked the street and crowds. "She's his mother."

A heartrending scream shook the world around them as the cars inched forward once more, signaled by the changing light.

Cade's body went rigid. The woman turned in the direction of the scream. A cocktail of dread and panic burned in his chest. He couldn't see her. Couldn't pinpoint where the sound was coming from. Across the street? Up the block?

The car seat swung and bounced in his grip as Gus freaked out.

"Help!" It was Lyndy's scream again, and Cade knew.

"She's in the alley." Between the gym and diner. He took two long strides forward, debating the best angle to dart into traffic when the weight of Gus's carrier hindered his steps.

He couldn't take a baby on a foot chase. Could he? To save his mother? To confront a killer? He swore long and loud.

He couldn't run with Gus. And he couldn't leave him.

Something dragged against his arm.

"Go." The woman said, gripping the carrier beside his hand. "Go!" Her children gathered around her, along with a growing crowd outside the Sunshine Smoothie. "I'll take him inside. Out of the cold. He'll be safe," she insisted, tugging Gus's carrier once more. "Help her." Her eyes burned with determination and fear. "Go."

Cade released the carrier.

He launched himself into the street, racing for the alley, terrified of what he'd find and horrified by what he'd done. He'd left Gus with a stranger. The act had been a bullet cutting through his chest.

"Hurry!" A girl on a cell phone waved to Cade from the mouth of the alley. "He's got her. I've called 911! Hurry!"

Cade skidded around the corner between old

buildings where shadows hung thick and long, leaving only a small strip of light at the alley's center. The air was stale and wet like mud and moss and weeks of old trash. Worse than that was the dark figure ahead of him. One arm around Lyndy's middle and one hand across her mouth as he struggled to drag her backward.

Cade strode forward, fire raging in his core. "Let her go or I will shoot you," he seethed, his voice low and deadly serious. He flipped the snap on a holster nestled against his back and relieved it of its weapon.

The assailant slowed, probably weighing his options. He didn't appear armed. Was a head and shoulders taller than Lyndy, though only slightly broader. He wore black shoes, pants and a hoodie. His face was covered in a matching, thin, stretchy mask.

Cade raised his weapon without losing step. "She's not much to hide behind. I've got a clear shot of your head. And I never miss."

The man yanked Lyndy off her feet, raising her higher on his body, eliminating Cade's shot. He considered the man's legs, ankles or feet. All were solid options, though smaller and moving more rapidly than his head. A hit would take him down, but be admittedly less satisfying.

"You've got nowhere to go," Cade taunted, smug satisfaction growing in his chest.

The assailant turned his head left and right, likely looking for an escape route, but there was none that Cade could see.

He lengthened his strides, eating up the distance between them. "Release her and you can live. Test your luck. You. Will. Lose."

Lyndy closed her eyes and grabbed the arm across her middle with both her hands. She pulled her knees up in a crunch, then straightened them with a roar and a grunt. Her feet connected with her abductor's shins, and a wail of pain burst free from him.

He stumbled back, arms flung wide for balance, only to snake an arm out and catch her by her hair as she stumbled to regain her footing on the broken concrete and asphalt.

Cade struggled for a clear shot as Lyndy wailed, clutching at her head where he'd grabbed her.

She flew suddenly forward, tossed and skidding over the filthy, slush-covered ground. The scream that had erupted from her core struck instantly silent as she collided headfirst into the nearby brick wall. The impact was audible.

Chapter Eleven

Lyndy's teeth chattered despite the layers of blankets wrapped around her coat and shoulders. Misplaced, or leftover, adrenaline thrummed in her system as the EMT added two stitches to the cut on her forehead. She hadn't blacked out, thankfully. Hadn't gotten a concussion, but the pain had been excruciating as she'd hit the rough and unforgiving brick with a hellacious whack. Her vision had blurred, maybe from the impact, maybe from the tears, and she'd collapsed in silence as the pain stole her breath. But Cade had been there to pick her up.

Now her throbbing head was only one of her many parts wishing for aspirin, ice and a bed. Her neck and shoulders were whiplashed. Her back was achy and sore. Her hands and knees were scraped and bleeding, though at least the wounds had been cleaned and treated by a paramedic with an angel's soft touch.

Cade paced several feet away, clearly livid and fresh out of patience. He barked at local law enforcement officers, federal agents and a growing number of bystanders who he thought should've done more to catch Lyndy's attacker before he'd disappeared. Apparently, the back door of one building in the alley made an excellent escape hatch, and the attacker had fled after nearly knocking a woman's head off. He was long gone by the time police arrived. Cade had been forced to choose between chasing the bad guy and caring for Lyndy. He'd chosen her, and her heart had cracked irreparably open for him. A pain she would surely deal with later.

Despite Cade's frustration that citizens hadn't given chase for him, many had rushed to help provide triage and countless others had called 911 when they'd heard Lyndy scream. According to her angelic EMT, the lines had been jammed with reports of Lyndy's abduction. Thanks to local media coverage following Carmen's attack, everyone was on the alert for the Kentucky Tom Cat Killer, so they were quick to call but slow to act. Perfectly understandable to Lyndy, who wasn't convinced she'd have tried to take on a potential serial killer if the tides had been turned. Cade was, clearly, less forgiving.

She homed in on the local news crew that had set up just outside the perimeter established by the police. The crew had nearly beaten officers to the scene, and she couldn't help wondering if they knew more than she did at this point about what had happened.

"The Tom Cat Killer has escalated," the reporter in a navy suit and festive tie explained to the camera. "He's got one local woman on his mind, and he's desperate to have her. Proof? He struck again today, right here in this familiar downtown alley, an off-shoot of Main Street, amidst a brood of holiday shoppers. But the people of our community responded with a resounding no!" He paused for dramatic effect, and Lyndy felt another welling of tears. She loved and appreciated Piedmont's sense of community in a crisis, but she hated being a victim.

The paramedic handed her a small plastic cup with a pair of painkillers in the bottom, then opened a bottle of water for her to wash them down. "You're going to be all right," the older woman said, her thick black hair worn in a braid that resembled a halo around her head. She smiled warmly and nodded. "This too shall pass. Remember that."

"Thank you," Lyndy whispered, taking the pills and wiping her eyes for the millionth time.

"I call them as I see them. That's all," the paramedic said, her voice thick with sincerity and concern. "You're shaken right now. You're hurting and afraid. Rightfully so. But whoever this Tom Cat is, he's just a man, and you've got a whole lot working on your side. For one, he's been called out, and everyone's watching. We're not going to let a wolf into the henhouse without a fight. And that man of yours looks more than capable of taking care of business than anyone I've seen in my life."

Lyndy glanced at Cade, who had Gus pinned to his chest, hugged tight in a sling made for her, a woman half his size. The murderous look he threw at the reporter, while wearing the baby in a too-small polka-dotted sling, did something to her insides. Despite everything else, she smiled. A moment later he headed in her direction, waving a hand absently while apparently talking to Gus.

"I want you to take this for pain," the EMT instructed. "Plenty of rest and fluids. Ice your neck and shoulders as needed." She handed Lyndy a prescription. "At least twice a day for the next few days. You'll heal faster if you aren't hurting."

Detective Owens arrived at the open ambulance doors a few steps before Cade. "How's she doing, Marla?" he asked the paramedic.

"She's going to be just fine."

Cade scoffed.

Marla smiled kindly and patted his arm. "You'll keep her safe, and Detective Owens will find that man. I have faith."

Cade slid his eyes to Lyndy. "Yes, ma'am." He helped Lyndy out of the ambulance and wrapped a protective arm across her back.

Overcome with need, she rolled against him, pressing her cheek against the warm contours of his chest and wrapping an arm over her baby in the little sling.

"I've got you," he whispered against the top of her head, pulling her into a strong and protective embrace. "I'm so sorry I let that happen."

Detective Owens cleared his throat, and Lyndy

jumped. His expression was judgmental, bordering on hostile, as she stepped away from Cade. She wanted to tell Cade that what happened wasn't his fault. That no one could've seen Tom coming. The whole thing had happened so fast. He'd been waiting in the hall outside the ladies' room, wearing a ski mask and pointing at something hidden under his jacket. He'd said he had a gun. Threatened to shoot someone waiting with the crowd by the register if she didn't go quietly. And no one had paid any attention as he'd nearly pushed her across the street. It wasn't until he'd repositioned the small metal bar beneath his coat that she'd realized he didn't have a gun. And she'd screamed.

"I've got Ramona Tinner's contact information from the diner," Owens said. "I'm headed there now while the feds finish here. I'm sending a cruiser to the Wells residence, and I'll keep a unit in position full-time. I'd appreciate it if you stay in touch with them and with me."

"Yes, sir," she said, feeling inexplicably guilty as the older man walked away.

CADE FED AND played with Gus until the baby fell asleep. There was something oddly comforting about caring for him. Maybe it was the fact Cade had done such a terrible job keeping Lyndy safe today, which made seeing her baby smile all the more reassuring. Maybe it meant he wasn't a total failure at something he'd been charged with doing this week.

He'd spoken to the members of his team several times and been told at length that he'd done nothing wrong. That the timing had simply been perfect on Tom's end, but Cade couldn't relieve the nagging sensation that there was more he should've done. Instead, the serial killer had only needed Cade to let his guard down for a moment, and Cade had. He couldn't let that happen again. There was no room for error. Tom had proven that yet again, and Lyndy had paid the price.

At least his caring for Gus gave Lyndy an opportunity to shower and rest. Though he doubted she'd sleep well tonight after what she'd been through. He wouldn't blame her. Given the last week of her life. In all honesty, he wasn't sure how she'd ever sleep soundly again, even after the monster had been caught. Not until Gus was grown.

Caring for the infant all afternoon and evening had already done something to Cade that he wasn't sure he'd recover from. He'd removed the baby from the sling only to realize an invisible tether had formed between them, linking the chubby, toothless infant straight to Cade's heart. More shocking, still, was the misplaced feeling of personal responsibility sure to extend beyond Cade's limited time in the child's life. He'd already wondered multiple times if Lyndy might allow him to come back and visit once in a while. He wanted to see Gus learn to walk, ride a bike, play T-ball and Little League. He shook the irrational thoughts away as soon as they came, but they lingered on the periphery of his mind, never far and always quick to return.

Thoughts of the child's mother were the same. Would she want to see Cade again when this was over? Did he want that? If he didn't, then why couldn't he stop thinking about it?

A door creaked open at the end of the hallway, followed by a soft set of footfalls. Lyndy appeared a moment later, looking sheepish and wearing a pale pink T-shirt and white cotton shorts. Her feet were bare, her toenails red, and her hair was slightly mussed. She looked like something pulled straight from Cade's favorite fantasy. Except this woman was real, and she'd been hurt today. She'd been attacked twice this week, and there were stitches along the red and swollen skin of her hairline to prove it. Her knees and palms were scraped and raw, only just beginning to scab. And suddenly all he wanted to do was scoop her off her feet and hold her until this nightmare was over.

"Hey," he said, his voice coming lower and thicker than intended. "How are you doing?"

She crossed her arms over her chest and Cade's protective PG thoughts took a turn.

The room was a little chilly, and she obviously hadn't been sleeping in a bra.

"Couldn't rest," she said. "How's Gus?"

"Out cold," Cade said with a swell of pride, pointing to the playpen he'd converted into a makeshift crib. "I hated to put him in his room where I couldn't see him, so I thought this would work for tonight."

Her sweet mouth curled at the edge as she moved toward her son. "Thank you."

Cade forced his attention away from her lush lips, short shorts and lucky pink top. "Can I get you something?" he asked. already moving toward the counter. "Water, coffee, tea? Are you hungry?"

"Just sore," she said, touching a hand to her forehead. "The pain pills knocked out the worst of it, but my palms and knees itch where they're scraped. I couldn't get comfortable in any of my pajama pants."

His gut twisted, and the urge to hold her hit again. The image of Detective Owens's disapproving expression held him at bay. It had been a well-needed reminder that Cade's thoughts and behaviors were crossing a line where Lyndy and Gus were concerned. And it wasn't fair to them.

"On second thought, maybe I should have some water," she said, moving in his direction. She tipped her head side to side and rubbed at the bunched muscles along her shoulders. "And another pain pill. I feel like I was hit by a bus."

Cade filled a glass with ice and water, then passed it to her. "You're a warrior. That's the second time you bested him."

"Well, desperate times," she said hoarsely before sipping the water, brows furrowed. "I was in a helpless panic until you pulled a gun and started threatening him. Seeing you made me brave."

"I'm glad." Cade passed her a pill from the prescription he'd insisted they have filled on the way home, and waited while she took it with another sip from her glass. "You're supposed to take that with food. How do you feel about grilled cheese?"

"You don't have to do that," she said, gripping the back of her neck. "I can throw a slice of bread in the toaster."

"And I can make grilled cheese."

She rolled her eyes. "Then, thank you."

Cade got to work on the sandwich as Lyndy padded back in Gus's direction.

"He looks so peaceful," she said. "I'm sorry you were stuck babysitting today. Now you're making meals and administering pills. I hate that you're doing all this extra stuff and I'm doing nothing."

"I'm not stuck, and this isn't extra," he said. "I'm going to see you through this. You and Gus. Whatever you need. For as long as it takes." He just hoped he could bring himself to leave when the job ended. He might be good at grilled cheese and watching her baby, but he wasn't good for her. He didn't stick with anyone long term for a reason. His dad had been a special kind of awful, and Cade didn't want to accidentally follow in his old man's footsteps, ruining the lives of those closest to him. He might be a better man, or he might not, but he refused to test the waters on Lyndy. She deserved more and better.

The tension in Lyndy's posture had disappeared

by the time her sandwich was gone, along with the lines between her brows.

"Feeling better?" he asked.

"Definitely." She carried her empty glass to the sink, then stared through the window into the darkness.

"Maybe now you'll be able to sleep."

"Maybe." She rolled her shoulders and stretched her muscles. "The pills are working. The pain's gone, but my muscles are still tight."

"May I?" he asked, moving around to stand behind her.

Her eyes met his in the reflection of the glass, reminding him of the moment they'd shared at her gym. "Yes."

He brushed the hair away from her neck with the tips of his fingers, then grazed his palms along her tender flesh. He pressed gently on her shoulders, allowing the pads of his thumbs to caress her nape and watching her expression in the glass for signs of discomfort.

Her head fell back against his chest with a soft groan. Eyes closed, lips parted as he worked the remaining tension from her muscles. Despite all she'd been through. She trusted him.

"Better?" he asked.

Her eyes drifted lazily open. "That's amazing."

He smiled at the breathless words. "Thanks."

"Is it wrong that I wouldn't mind knowing what else your hands could do for me?"

Cade barked a laugh, but his body responded

instantly and powerfully to the possibilities. "Not wrong," he said, "but I have a feeling that's the pain pill talking."

She turned lithely in the small space between the sink and his body, rubbing her warm breasts against him as she stretched onto her toes and fitted her hands behind his head. "I'm feeling much better now."

"I see that," he said, setting his hands against the gentle curve of her waist and allowing himself a moment of selfish indulgence. She smiled, and he slid his hands over the curves of her hips before drawing his fingers back up, tracing the line of her spine.

She shivered, and he moaned.

Lyndy tipped her head back and locked him in her heated blue gaze. "I like the way you touch me."

"How do I touch you?" he asked taking baby steps backward, leading her toward the hall.

"Like my body is a treasure."

His smile widened. "Not your body," he whispered against the narrow curve of her ear. "You. And I think it's time I take you back to bed." He hooked one arm behind her knees before lifting her off the ground and carrying down the hall. "Don't get any ideas," he warned, speaking to Lyndy as much as himself. "I'm only going to tuck you in."

Her bottom lip jutted out in disappointment. "Will you kiss me good-night?"

"Not this time, Sleeping Beauty."

But he hoped that maybe one day he could.

Chapter Twelve

Lyndy woke rested but sore when the pain medication wore off, and the effects of her most recent attack ruined her peace. She eased upright, then shuffled to the bathroom in preparation for her day. Tantalizing aromas of bacon and eggs floated down the hall on a chorus of Gus's laughter. Lyndy smiled. Despite it all, Gus was safe and happy, and that was all that mattered.

She climbed into the shower and lingered beneath the searing spray until her skin was as red as a sunburn and the water had loosened her aching muscles. When the throbbing pain in her head demanded she get out, Lyndy toweled off and pulled a cotton t-shirt over her head. She chose a wide, stretchy headband to keep her hair away from her face. More important, away from the angry, puckered wound on her forehead. She dabbed ointment on the itchy stitches and then concealer over the unsightly bruises along her cheek and jawbone. The mascara and lip gloss were administered in sheer defiance. An attempt to feel more like herself and less like the Tom Cat's little mouse.

Finished, she hurried down the hall to see Gus and pour some coffee. She refused to think about how much she wanted to see Cade, too. "Good morning, pumpkin" she called, rounding the corner in a bee-line for her baby in his highchair.

Gus cooed and babbled at the sight of her. Cade had dressed him in a black T-shirt and jeans with white socks. "What are you wearing?" she asked, kissing his chubby fingers and the bottoms of his kicking feet.

"What's wrong with what he's wearing?" Cade asked, stepping in from the living room and pocketing his phone.

"He looks like a greaser."

Cade frowned, and Lyndy noticed with a smile that Cade was essentially wearing the same outfit, though his T-shirt was a V-neck and Gus's shirt had a little pocket. "What do you mean?"

She filled a mug with coffee and suppressed a laugh. A little ball rolled against her foot, and she realized part of the kitchen floor was covered in them. "What happened in here?"

Cade scooped a red, white and blue stress ball from the floor and set it on Gus's tray. "We're training."

Gus flung his arms until the ball went over the tray's edge, then squealed and clapped his hands together.

"Gus wants to be a professional pitcher," Cade explained, "if football doesn't work out."

"Ah." Lyndy sipped her coffee and smiled. "That's quite a plan."

"Well, it's important to have dreams," Cade said, tossing and catching one of the squishy balls. "Fortress Defense swag. I found a bag of them in the truck."

"Did you go out?" Lyndy asked, feeling a shard of fear slice through her at the idea she and Gus had been alone.

"No. I was looking for a bag of surveillance equipment I normally keep on hand. I think it's at the office, so I'm going to need to make a run back home. I left in too big of a hurry when Owens called."

She bit her lip, a fresh wave of guilt riding over her. Now he was tied up indefinitely and dealing with a serial killer. She turned for the bottle of pain pills on her windowsill and cracked it open.

Cade smiled.

"What?"

He shook his head. "Nothing. Did you sleep okay?"

"Yeah." She removed a pill and used a paring knife to break it in half. A whole pill had put her to sleep so deeply last night that she didn't remember going to bed. She couldn't afford to conk out like that again until after dinner. Until then, she'd do her best to be useful if yesterday's attack had generated any leads.

Cade watched her carefully as she took half the pill and returned the rest to the bottle. She appreciated the concern in his soulful blue eyes. "How are you feeling?"

"Okay. Sore and scared. Sorry you were dragged into this, but thankful you're here."

He smiled "Yeah?"

"Yeah."

Gus pounded the highchair tray, and Lyndy gripped her forehead. "That pill has not kicked in yet."

Cade loaded Gus's tray with stress balls, then pulled out a chair at the table for Lyndy. "How about some bacon?"

Lyndy ate greedily while a torrent of questions blew around her mind. "If you hadn't been with me yesterday, I would've had Gus when Tom took me."

Cade's level expression met hers. "I know."

"You can't stay with us forever, so what are we going to do?" she asked, hating again that the first part was true.

His frown deepened. "Let's concentrate on today. For starters, I thought we could decorate your Christmas tree together after dinner. I put it up while you were asleep. Just the tree and lights. All the ornaments are still in the totes. We can string popcorn. Maybe watch that movie I've been trying to get to. Something fun for the holiday?"

She paused, a strip of bacon at her lips. "You put up my tree?"

"Is that okay?"

She pushed onto her feet and went to see for herself. Sure enough, her mother's thirty-year-old artificial tree had been assembled near the front window. Her homemade, childhood tree skirt fanned out beneath it. Rows of chasing colored lights danced and flashed erratically below a star made of cardboard and tinfoil. A star she'd made in preschool and her mother had cherished. Sam had insisted she leave it in storage and use an antique glass star of his family's, instead. "Thank you," she said, breathless with appreciation. "It's perfect."

Cade smiled. "While you're so happy with me, what do you think about a road trip this morning?"

"Back to Fortress?" she guessed, remembering his comment about needing to go home.

"If you're up to it. I'd like to pick up some supplies and possibly another team member, if that's all right with you."

Lyndy gave the tree and star another look. "I'd love to."

She bit into her third slice of bacon, contemplating her life.

"Penny for your thoughts?" Cade asked, pouring a mug of coffee and taking the seat across from her.

"I had a really normal life last week," she mused, wondering if the pain pill was kicking in. "Small, but comfortable. A little lonely, but I was happy. I'm not sure how I got from there to here. Now my face is on the morning, evening and nightly news. Some psychotic murderer is after me. I've got a bodyguard living with me and a police detail outside."

Cade frowned. "What were your days like before? What would you be doing right now if none of this had happened?"

"What do you mean?" she asked, turning intentionally away from the pile of bacon before she took another slice.

"You wouldn't be making a road trip with your bodyguard to collect weapons, surveillance materials and a second man for your protection," he said. "So what would you be doing instead?"

"Well," Lyndy began, slightly stumped. It had only been a few days, but that small, quiet life she'd just mentioned seemed so far away now. "I guess I'd be at work." She checked the clock on the wall for confirmation. "If none of this had happened, I would've gotten up at five thirty. Gotten myself ready, then Gus. I'd have grabbed a granola bar on the way out the door at seven and taken him to day care by seven thirty before racing across town to work by eight."

"Where you interview folks who need employment?" Cade asked.

"Correct."

"You like it?"

Lyndy smiled. No one had ever asked her that before. "I like the people," she said. "I like knowing I can help folks."

He shifted in his seat, stretching long legs beneath the table. "After work?"

"I pick Gus up. We walk at the park, then head home. We do our nighttime routine after dinner and he's usually asleep by nine. I read until I fall asleep, too."

"When do you go out with your friends?" Cade asked.

She shook her head, suddenly feeling a little sorry for herself. "No friends." The busyness of her life had made it seem so full. She hadn't realized how solitary she'd become. Not like now, with Cade there to talk to, share meals and laugh with even when she wanted to cry. "What about you?"

"I love what I do," Cade answered.

"Is this what you'd be doing on a normal work day?" she asked, curious now. What were his other cases like comparatively? "Making clients' breakfast and coaching infants for a career in professional baseball?"

"Wait a minute. Baseball only happens if football fails," he said with a wink that made her grin.

Lyndy waited, desperate for more information about his life and clients before her. She wanted to know this assignment was different. Not because of the circumstances, but because of her.

Cade watched Gus for a long beat before answering. "I'd be outside the home monitoring the perimeter at this time of day. Or maybe in my truck outside the client's office while they worked. I normally keep my distance. I try to blend into the background of my clients' lives so they feel safe without having to explain why I'm there to everyone they know."

"That seems…" Lyndy struggled to find the word "…sad." She offered a weak smile.

"It's not sad. It's the job."

"Okay, so when do you get to feel like you belong instead of like you shouldn't be seen?" she asked.

"Between jobs. Anytime I'm back at Fortress."

"Do you spend a lot of time with your teammates then?" she asked, trying not to sound so deeply interested.

"No." Something in his tone seemed off, as if he was noticing the same thing she was. They both had lives built wholly around something they loved. And somewhere along the line, they'd each given themselves up for the cause. Her thing was Gus. Cade's was his job. But was that enough? For now? Forever?

His brows tented. "We stay busy. There's often more jobs than we can take on. We're looking to expand, add to the team, but it takes time to vet potential employees when we're already gone more days than we're home."

Lyndy's heart broke for him. Was it possible he was surrounded by people he cared about and just as lonely as she was?

Cade cleared his throat and stood, collecting their empty plates. "I need to make some notes about your property before we go. It'll help with the supplies and planning. Feel like a quick walk?"

"Sounds good." She bundled Gus then grabbed her coat and joined Cade outside a few minutes later, where they examined the land she'd bought with Sam. Everything about it looked different now. Without him. Without the grief. With a finally healed heart, she could truthfully say this property was never what she'd wanted. And once this mess was over, she was going to sell it and move.

"I've covered most of the ground and pulled up details from your county auditor's site," Cade said, slipping into a sort of businessman mode she hadn't seen before. "But those sites are often outdated, and they don't include the details human can provide. So, what can you tell me about your land?"

Lyndy breathed in the fresh morning air and surveyed the vast spread before her. "There's 8.9 acres. The road out front is the only way in. The property butts up against four others. One on each side and two behind. Those properties are all larger. Two have homes. Two don't. The nearest home is nearly a half mile away." *A quick walk, but too far for them to hear her scream*, she thought morbidly.

"Neighbors?" he asked.

"I've never met them. The home to the south is part of a dairy farm. The house next door belongs to an elderly couple who don't get out much."

"What about outbuildings?"

"Just the two in the backyard. The old barn is decrepit. Sam planned to restore it, but it seems like a death trap to me. The small building was going to be my henhouse." She smiled at the sweet thought. "All I've ever wanted was a nice little backyard with a grill and a swing set. Someplace I could enjoy my grandmama's sweet tea and watch my kids play. Funny how perfect that sounds when you're young and the world's still full of possibilities."

Cade looked from her face to Gus's and then back. "I think it sounds nice. So how'd you end up with all this if you only wanted a small yard and a henhouse?"

She shrugged, adjusting Gus in his sling. "I met Sam when he was in my hometown on business. We dated, then got engaged quickly. My mom had just died, and my grandmama not long before her. My dad's always been absentee, so I was alone and didn't want to be. Sam was nice, so I left everything I knew and came here to be with him. Now he's gone and I'm alone. With Gus, of course, but irony, right?"

Cade didn't answer, but his searching gaze sent chills over her skin. He turned back toward the house and set a heavy palm against the small of her back to guide her along with him.

The gentle pressure of his fingers sent shock waves through her core. She wanted to know what those fingers felt like beneath the coat. On her skin. In her hair.

Cade opened the back door for her and locked up behind them once they stepped inside.

She removed a sleeping Gus from his sling and coat, then crept down the hall to his room and nestled him in his crib. She gripped the tensing muscles along her neck as she made her way back to Cade in the kitchen. "I expected the headache," she said, absently reaching for a bottle of aspirin in the cupboard, "but I can't get over how much everything else aches. Do you think I can take these with the prescription?"

"Why not take the other half of your pill?" he asked with a gleam in his eye.

She wrinkled her nose. "The painkillers I took after Gus was born made me goofy, and I don't even remember going to bed last night. I have to wait until we're in for the night before I take a full pill again."

Cade grinned. "Define goofy."

Her cheeks heated with the humiliating memories. "I said anything I wanted, usually the minute it came to mind and completely without filter. I told the man delivering my pizza that his breath stank and a mother breastfeeding her baby on a park bench that she was a hero."

His grin widened. "So the pills are like truth serum?"

She felt her jaw drop. "Did I say something last night?"

He shrugged, a wicked expression on his handsome face. "To clarify," he said, stepping into her personal space. "You always say exactly what you mean when you take the pills?"

"Unfortunately."

He chuckled, then raised his palms and brows in

question. "I can help with the muscle tension. Do you trust me?"

"Implicitly."

His mouth parted and his gaze darkened as he set his broad hands against her shoulders, pulling her closer and working his fingers carefully over the tender skin. "The tugging and tight feeling you have is probably caused by spasms. They're common after a trauma and are normally painful, but the prescription you're taking is knocking the edge off. I'm going to try to relax the muscles so they stop gripping and releasing."

Lyndy's breath caught as his hands slid down the length of her arms, then moved to the curves of her waist, his strong steady fingers massaging the muscles of her back. Her head rolled over one shoulder as his hands glided up her spine and between her shoulder blades, probing and testing, expertly releasing the painful knots of tension.

"I have another idea," he said, stepping away. "Be right back."

Lyndy couldn't imagine what he was up to, but if it was going to feel half as good as that back massage, she was all in.

Cade swaggered back a moment later, a tube of cream in his hand. "My sergeant introduced me to this after I rolled my jeep in Kabul. I still use it when I overdo my workouts. It's warm at first, but it's great for muscle pain." He lifted a hand tentatively to her shoulder. "May I?"

Lyndy bit into her bottom lip, nearly vibrating with anticipation of his touch.

He stepped close again, the scent, heat and presence of him flooding into her senses as he curled his hands over the slope of her shoulders and tugged the wide V-neck of her T-shirt off one shoulder.

She released an involuntary moan of pleasure as the cool cream hit her skin, then froze as an intrusive and fuzzy memory presented itself, effectively ruining the moment. "Did you rub my neck last night?" she asked, knowing the truth, remembering with sudden clarity how perfectly delicious his touch had felt and how badly she'd wanted more.

Cade pulled his hands away, as if he'd done something wrong. "Yes."

She covered her mouth, recalling the things she'd been thinking. The fantasies she'd been enjoying. "I was doped up on that pain pill." And she'd wanted him to touch her. She'd asked him to kiss her goodnight. But he hadn't.

"I stopped the moment I realized," he said. "I put you in bed. Alone."

Lyndy added *honorable* to the growing list of reasons she was falling hard and fast for her protector. Before she could say so, the scent of the uncapped lotion in his raised hand brought a rush of other, more awful memories to the surface. "Oh my goodness."

"Nothing happened. I swear."

"No." She grabbed the tube from Cade, her hand shaking hard against his and inhaled deeply. Instantly, the dark lake at the park flashed into mind. The slip of her feet on wet grass. The pressure of an arm on her body. A hand on her mouth. "He smelled like this." She blinked against a rush of unbidden tears. "Cade. The man who grabbed me smelled exactly like this!"

Chapter Thirteen

Cade dialed Detective Owens as Lyndy moved away, her breaths coming shuddered and quick.

She collapsed onto a kitchen chair, cheeks pale as he waited for the call to connect.

"Hey. This is good," he promised, crouching before her to look into her eyes. "You've just come across the most viable clue the police have had in months. This is better than good," he amended. "It might be the break they need to finally name this lunatic."

Lyndy nodded, whether in understanding or agreement, he wasn't sure.

He stood and squeezed her shoulder gently as he listened to the infuriating rings of a call going unanswered. Pressure grew in his gut. Linking this scent to the killer was big. No one used muscle cream unless they needed it. Whoever the feds had on their suspect list could be narrowed significantly with this. "Come on, Owens. Pick up," he muttered.

The gentle pressure of Lyndy's small hand on his

unfurled something in his core. She'd set her palm over his hand on her shoulder and curled her thin fingers around his for support. The simple gesture was so sweet, so innocent and so wholly welcome that his leathery heart gave a heavy thump. *She* was comforting *him*. Even in a moment when she was speechless. No one had ever done that before. Cade had always been the strong one. The provider for his siblings. A warrior for his country. The Fortress member always on assignment so the others could be with their loved ones. Nothing and no one in his life had ever been about him. All his present and past relationships had been based on what he could do for someone else.

The sound of Detective Owens's recorded voice mail message pulled Cade back to the moment. "No answer," he said, his voice unexpectedly rough. He turned the phone around and dialed again, only to receive the same result. This time he cleared his throat and left a message.

"Detective Owens," he began, unable to hide his irritation. He needed to speak to the man himself. "This is Cade Lance. Lyndy Wells has something I think you and the feds can run with on the Tom Cat case. She's identified the scent of the man who attempted to abduct her. It's a muscle cream called Hayden's Own. It's holistic, no chemicals, just oils and extracts, with a unique eucalyptus and lemongrass scent. It's hard to find, and it's not sold nationally. I'm willing to bet it was bought locally." He freed his hand from Lyndy's and paced as his temper grew. "The manager at the Sunshine Smoothie wore a sling. I'd like to verify his injury, the cause and timeline."

Lyndy's distant gaze snapped up to meet his, and she sucked in a deep, ragged breath.

"That guy told me he had a torn rotator cuff, but I'm starting to think a sling and exaggerated injury are the perfect ways to make a guilty man seem innocent." It was possible that an injured manager at the most likely location to host Lyndy's stalker wasn't the man they were looking for, but it made for some strong coincidences. Cade didn't believe in coincidences.

Lyndy pushed onto her feet, looking ill. She darted to the sink and turned on the water as Cade disconnected the call. She pulled a rag from the drawer and pumped soap from the dispenser then began to scrub her shoulder in short, frantic strokes. Removing the small amount of cream he'd applied.

Cade pocketed the phone on his way to the sink. "Lyndy." He shut the water off and pried the rag from her fisted hand, saving the red and swelling skin, which she'd rubbed to excess, from any further abuse. "Hey," he said more softly, pulling her into his embrace. "I've got you."

She pressed her forehead to his chest and curled her fingers into the fabric of his shirt. "I hate him," she whispered. "Why can't they stop him?"

"Me, too," he said, "and they will." Cade stroked

her back and folded her deeper into his protective embrace. "I won't let him hurt you again." He felt the truth of the words in his marrow. No one would hurt Lyndy again, not without going through him first, and no one got through Cade.

She eased her head back and leveled him with a warm, trusting gaze. "Okay."

He smiled. "Just like that, huh?"

"Yeah." She forced a tight smile, but made no move to release him. "I didn't mean to freak out. That smell just…"

"That smell will probably always make you sick now," he said, knowing firsthand how strongly the sense of scent was tied to memories. There were a number of things he'd prefer to never smell again. Diesel exhaust in the desert. Freshly turned earth. The cloying scent of too many flowers on caskets of men too young to have gone home in them. "But it won't always be so intense or scary when the memories come. Time will make that easier." Time and knowing the son of a gun was locked up for life.

Lyndy wet her lips and slowly uncurled her fingers, releasing the material of his shirt. "Thanks for saying that. Logically, I know Gus and I are safe, and that the outside threat won't last forever, but sometimes it just feels like too much. Like this is our life now, and we'll never be safe again." She flattened her palms against the wrinkled material on his chest then slid her hands up and over his shoulders, bringing their bodies tightly together once more. "It's nice to feel anchored again."

Anchored. The word reminded him of the invisible tether he'd imagined between himself and Gus. That undeniable connection was looped tightly around Lyndy, too. He cupped her sweet face in his hands, searching for the words to thank her for reminding him he was more than a bodyguard, more than a former marine, more than a vessel moving from duty to duty. He was a man who wanted things for himself, like a home and a family. A man who wanted *her*.

Before he could verbalize his gratitude, Lyndy rose onto her toes. Without breaking eye contact, she dusted her lips gently across his in a touch so light it might've been her breath if he hadn't felt the aftershocks of it in his core. She pulled back slightly when he didn't reciprocate.

Need burned in him as he deliberated. He wasn't supposed to want her. Not in his arms, in his bed, or in his future, but right now, with her looking at him like that, it took all his remaining self-control not to take her mouth with his. She deserved more than a man who'd take advantage of her while she was in danger. And he didn't want to be a distraction from her fear or a temporary anchor in the storm.

Lyndy's cheeks reddened as he held her in place, turning scarlet with humiliation. "I'm so sorry." She slid her hands off him and lowered slowly from her toes. She pressed her lips tight and averted her gaze. "I misread the situation. I was out of line." She turned quickly away.

Cade followed, pulled by the tether. "Wait." He snaked out an arm to stop her, unsure what to say next. He couldn't explain the chaos and confusion raging in his heart and mind. There weren't words, and it wasn't right. Not now. Not until her life was her own again and she could make clear decisions, unaffected by external circumstances.

She spun on him, and he rocked back on his heels. Her chin rose in defiance. "It's fine. I'm fine. The truth is that I think you're handsome and kind, and I feel connected to you. It's peaceful and exhilarating and really very confusing. Maybe it's the extenuating circumstances. I don't think so, but I don't know. And honestly, I can't say that I care. I've wanted you since the moment I set eyes on you, and that isn't like me at all."

Cade's muscles seized as her words hit like missiles to his heart.

"It's okay that you don't want me, too," she continued. "I'll get over it, and I promise not to try that again, but please don't go. I don't think I can get through this without you."

Cade caught her chin in his hand and slid his palm against her cheek in a desperate caress. "I'm supposed to be here as your protector," he rasped.

A peppy country tune began suddenly, and Lyndy started.

He released her, and she dashed away, leaving a chill in her absence.

"That's my cell phone. It could be Detective Owens," she said, digging into her bag for the device. "Hello?"

Cade watched, willing his heart rate to slow and wishing equally that he could thank and throttle whoever was on the other end of the line.

"Okay," Lyndy said, alarm in her voice and on her brow. "I'll be right there." She pressed the phone to her chest and stared, horrified, at Cade. "That was my office. I just got a delivery."

LYNDY STROKED GUS's soft hair and peppered him with kisses, hating to wake him, especially for this reason. The last time they'd gone into town together, it hadn't ended well.

"Hi, sleepyhead," she whispered as his little lids dragged open, and his mouth pulled into an enormous yawn. "We're going to take a little trip." She lifted him into her arms and hugged him tight, wanting to infuse and fortify him with her love.

Cade shifted against the doorjamb, where he watched. "Anything I can do to help?"

"I've got this," she said, setting Gus on the changing table and willing the instant memory of Cade's rejection away. She'd said her piece. She'd told him she wanted him despite all sense and logic. And he'd told her he was only there as her protector. She'd done the brave thing by being honest, and he'd done the same in return.

Theirs was a working relationship.

"Did your office tell you what sort of delivery it was?" he asked.

"No." And she hadn't thought to ask. She changed Gus, then gave him a hearty snuggle before heading in Cade's direction.

He slid smoothly out of her way, careful not to touch her. "Do you normally receive deliveries at the office?"

"Sometimes," she admitted, though her company frowned on it. "I'm rarely home during the hours deliveries are made. I can't sign for anything here, and I'd hate to leave a package on the porch all day."

Lyndy made Gus a bottle, then tucked the makings of another into her bag in case they were in town longer than expected.

"Have you ordered anything recently?" Cade asked, sticking to her heels as she moved through the house.

"Not that I can recall, but I have standing orders for things I get often like diapers, formula and wipes." She paused to sigh. "Look, I'm having a bit of a day here, and whatever is waiting for me at the office is probably something awful. We both know that. So you might as well call Detective Owens back and leave another message."

Cade pursed his lips, brows furrowed.

Lyndy slid her feet into the ankle boots beside her

door. She'd changed into her softest jeans and white
tank top with a pale green sweater before waking
Gus. The ankle boots would go well with the ensemble while keeping her feet warm in the inch or
so of snow that had added up from the day's flur-
ries. "Let's just get this over with before I lose my
nerve." She turned the knob and waited, suddenly
immobilized by the thought of walking out alone.

"I've got it." Cade reached for the knob, forcing
her back, then motioned her onto the empty porch.

She wanted to sail dramatically down the steps
and across the lawn to his waiting truck but couldn't.
Instead she froze, scanning the wide-open space in
search of an assailant cloaked in black and coated
in muscle cream.

"Pretty day," Cade said, passing her on the porch.

Lyndy tried to appreciate the view. Endless blue
skies above snow-dusted fields and distant mountains rising in the background. The scene would've
been picture-perfect if her world wasn't falling apart.

The truck's locks popped up, and Cade opened her
door. Her palms were clammy as she buckled Gus
into the safety harness, and her knees were shaking
as she climbed onto the seat.

Cade stood silently for several long beats before
shutting the door behind her. He rounded the hood
with a troubled expression, then folded himself behind the wheel. "I'd like to hold your hand in town,"
he said, casting a furtive look in her direction. "If
you put Gus in the sling and I hold your hand, I'll

have the both of you within arm's reach and a free hand for my sidearm if needed."

"Of course." She buckled up while he ignited the engine.

The world blew by in a blur. The commute to her office went both as fast and as slowly as she'd ever known. Her mouth was dry and pasty with anticipation by the time they reached the stout five-story building on the edge of town.

"Ready?" Cade asked, pulling the glass door open for her to pass.

Lyndy wrapped her arms around Gus, and a blast of dry heat poured over her shoulders as she breached the threshold. She led the way to the welcome desk at the center of the first-floor lobby. A giant Christmas tree rose in the corner, covered in cheery holiday decor and sprinkled with paper tags shaped like angels. Names of local families in need were printed on one side of each angel and a massive box beside the tree held gifts already purchased by building employees for the family members. Lyndy still had to wrap her purchases before bringing them in.

The oversize welcome desk was lined in twinkle lights and silver garland. The security guard watched astutely as they approached. Anyone who entered the building needed a pass to get beyond the desk.

"Hi, James." She waved, and James stood. He was in his late fifties and often surly, but he kept people out who didn't have an appointment, and he seemed to know every employee in the building by name.

"Ms. Wells." He stood to greet her, taking pointed notice of Gus in his sling before lancing Cade with a near-threatening look. "New beau?" he asked, turning away before she answered.

Cade linked his hand with hers and gave her fingers an encouraging squeeze.

"He is," she said, hoping to sound light and carefree, though the bruising and stitches on her face would make the facade hard to pull off. "This is my boyfriend, Cade. Cade, this is James. He makes sure the entire building runs smoothly."

James gave Cade another look, cocking his head before suddenly standing straighter. "Military?"

"Yes, sir. Marines. You?"

"Air Force." James unbuttoned his shirtsleeve and rolled one cuff above his elbow. The letters USAF were inked on his skin.

Cade released Lyndy, then extended a hand to the older man. The pair gave one strong pump of their arms. When Cade released him, he raised that hand in salute. "Thank you for your service."

James's usually stern expression eased, and for a moment, emotion clouded his eyes. He returned the salute quickly, then looked to Lyndy with an approving smile. "Nice to see you found a good one." He issued their pass and took his seat with shoulders squared.

When they'd stepped onto the elevator, Lyndy pressed the button marked five and slid her eyes in

Cade's direction. "I see him every day, and he's never said more than hello to me."

Cade smiled. "He pegged me for military. Probably felt some camaraderie. It can be tough coming home after the service. Not everyone acclimates. Some never get a real footing."

"Did you?" she asked. He'd founded a successful business with his teammates, but had he really adjusted to being home? Had he even tried? From the way he'd described his life, it seemed like work was all he had, and that didn't seem like enough. Cade deserved to have more. To have whatever he wanted in life.

He stepped closer and set a hand against the small of her back. "I'm working on it."

The elevator doors parted, and the office receptionist nearly launched from her seat to greet Lyndy. "Oh my goodness! There you are!"

Cade moved away as Sylvia slung her arms around Lyndy and Gus, her silver pixie-cut hair and cat-eye glasses going slightly askew with the effort. "Oh, sweetie, look at you," she said, pulling back with a frown. Her gaze slipped over the bumps and bruises on Lyndy's face. "I am so sorry this is happening to you. None of us can believe it. You poor thing."

"I'm okay," Lyndy said, willing the words to be true.

Sylvia brushed a hand along Lyndy's arm, then squeezed her elbow. "Well, at least you aren't going through it alone." She slid her gaze in Cade's direction then back. "Hello, handsome. Am I right?" she asked, not bothering to quiet her voice. "Where on earth did you find him? Cause I'd like to stop there on my way home."

Lyndy laughed. "Sylvia, this is my boyfriend, Cade. Cade, meet Sylvia."

He stepped forward, one hand extended. "How do you do?"

Sylvia wrapped her arms around his solid core and pressed her cheek to his pecs. "Very well," she said. "Very, very well."

When Cade gave in and hugged her back, she lifted one peep-toed pump off the ground like a cartoon princess.

Lyndy laughed at Cade's shocked expression. "I believe you mentioned a delivery for me, Sylvia."

The older woman released Cade with a little goodbye pat to his abs. "I did." She hurried around her desk and grabbed a large vase of flowers positioned beside the stacks of mail and unopened boxes. "But now that I see you have this nice fella, I suppose they're from him."

Lyndy's gut clenched and her head felt light. Roses and carnations. Just like the bouquet delivered to Carmen at the hospital.

Cade's arm came protectively around her waist. "I didn't send those." He pulled his phone from his pocket, snapped a picture, then immediately began to dial.

Lyndy pulled the envelope free of the stems. It

was bulky and too heavy for the typical card insert. Her fingers trembled as she broke the seal and pushed the flap out of her way.

A name badge from the local diner fell onto the reception desk. The white plastic tag was splattered with crimson stains and engraved with the letters R-a-m-o-n-a.

The attached card was scripted in matching crimson letters.

See you soon.

Chapter Fourteen

Cade recognized the first uniform to arrive on scene.
Officer Sanchez had been with Detective Owens at
the hospital after Carmen's attack, and he'd located
the coveralls Tom had shed. The look on Sanchez's
face said he was just as unhappy as Cade, and there
was a strange comfort in that. It meant that he wanted
this guy caught, too.

Sanchez spoke with James at the front desk while
waiting for a second officer to arrive. As usual Tom
had gotten his message to Lyndy in broad daylight,
and no one knew anything.

Cade listened raptly as James relayed all he could
remember. A delivery man had brought the flowers
in a white logoed truck from a florist he recognized.
The delivery man was one he'd seen many times and
knew by name. A bright side, if there was one to
be found. The man left the flowers, and James had
called Lyndy's office. That was that.

Officer Sanchez promised to speak with the driver
and whoever took the delivery order after he'd fin-

ished speaking with Lyndy and her friend Sylvia, but that too was a bust. Sylvia knew even less than James. She'd picked up the flowers in the lobby then rode the elevator back upstairs to call Lyndy.

The front doors opened, and a second uniformed officer walked inside.

Cade tensed, irritation clawing at his already heated temper. "Where's Owens?" he asked Sanchez. "I called him twice before all this. I called a third time to let him know Lyndy had a delivery, and I called again once we knew what it was. He should be here."

Sanchez scoffed. "You're not the only problem we've got today, Lance. So chill out and let us work."

Cade's frame went rigid. "What's so important that he can't return the calls of a woman being stalked by a killer?"

Lyndy shot Cade a warning look, then moved into the officer's path. She cocked her head and bounced slightly, playing with Gus's little fingers. "What other problem do you have today?"

"Try turning on the news," Sanchez said, looking defeated. "Any channel." He shook his head as he pushed his way past them, joining the second officer at the welcome desk. The flowers, note and name tag had been bagged and labeled. The second officer was on a call.

Lyndy swiped her thumb over the screen of her cell phone, then navigated to a local news site.

Cade moved in for a look over her shoulder.

A breaking news bar scrolled along the bottom of the screen: Death on Campus.

Lyndy gasped, and Cade pulled her closer. "Oh no," she whispered, going soft and weak at his side. "The man at Sunshine Smoothie said he thought Ramona lived in off-campus housing near his sister."

Cade guided her to the nearest bench, eyes fixed on the scrolling feed. He remembered the guy's words. When he coupled that information with Ramona's bloody name tag, it wasn't hard to guess who the report was about or why.

Tom had silenced his only witness in a permanent way.

"He killed her because of me." The horror in Lyndy's eyes hit like a sledge to Cade's chest.

He lowered himself beside her and scanned the growing crowd on screen. No signs of the infamous black ball cap.

Detective Owens appeared on the live feed, moving purposefully alongside the strategically placed caution tape, backdropped by emergency lights and controlled chaos. Hordes of gaping students loomed on both sides of the flimsy barrier, staring, chatting and filming the scene with their phones.

A pair of officers and paramedics followed Owens away from the building. The officers tended to bystanders while the paramedics guided a gurney carrying a body bag to a van with the county coroner's logo.

Lyndy made a small choking sound, her expression stricken.

Cade rubbed her back. "Remember this isn't your fault."

"Isn't it?" she snapped, looking as forlorn and weary as any marine he'd ever seen.

"We talked about this," he reminded her. "This is all him. And you can't let yourself think otherwise."

She dropped her face into a waiting palm. "I can't believe this is happening."

"They're going to find him," Cade assured.

"Ramona was our only hope of finding out who paid for my smoothies last year. She was the link I needed."

"I know."

Sanchez looked up from the desk, having clearly been eavesdropping. "Owens said the same thing. He's been trying to nail her down for a talk since you made the connection. Then he found her this morning."

"So it is her?" Cade asked, leveling Sanchez with his most no-nonsense stare.

The officer turned back briefly and dipped his chin in confirmation.

Lyndy cuddled Gus, pressing her cheek to the top of his head. She rolled her eyes up to meet Cade's. "Does this feel like another direct link to Terri at Sunshine Smoothie, or am I reading too much into it?"

"No. I'm right with you." Cade pushed onto his feet. "Are you finished with us here?" he called to Sanchez.

"Yeah, but watch yourselves," Sanchez said with a grimace. "Call me direct if you need me."

Cade hoisted Lyndy onto her feet, then patted his pocket where the officer's card was tucked away. "Will do."

He followed her into the sunlight, then slid his hand into hers. "You think you can help me find that apartment building from the news?"

She nodded. "Maybe we can catch Owens there."

LYNDY MOVED TOWARD the crime scene in long, even strides, determined to hold herself together in the face of the tragedy she'd inadvertently caused. Gus was cooperative as ever, content to watch the flashing lights and rushing people. Unaffected by the blowing winds and falling snow.

Cade stuck close to their side, occasionally brushing a palm against her back or his arm against her arm as they moved. His cologne and very presence were both undeniable and comforting.

She kept her chin up and put one foot in front of the other, pretending she belonged there. A trick she'd picked up long ago. People in positions of authority only stopped those who looked confused or guilty. As long as she stayed in motion, appeared to be on a set trajectory, no one tried to stop her.

They passed knots and clusters of students and lookie-loos, amateur vloggers and a news crew as they dipped under the flimsy yellow caution tape, but few paid any attention as they headed up the walkway to the building where Ramona had been found.

They'd nearly breached the threshold when a female officer stepped into the foyer and started at the sight of them. "Ms. Wells. You shouldn't be here." Her tone was firm but calm. There was a gentleness in her eyes that nearly buckled Lyndy's knees. "This is a restricted area."

Lyndy opened her mouth to speak, but the words failed. Officer Lee had been on traffic duty the night Sam died. She'd arrived at the door with her hat in hand and delivered the devastating news with a directness Lyndy had never forgotten. Her tone had been kind then, too, her words straight and piercing as arrows. When she'd learned Lyndy didn't have any family, Officer Lee had shown up at the memorial service and stood at Lyndy's side until the end. It was the last time they'd spoken.

"I'm Detective Lee," the officer said, offering her hand to Cade. "I'm sorry, but it's authorized personnel only beyond this point."

"Cade Lance," he said. "Detective Owens called me in to look after Lyndy and Gus. We've got information we think he needs."

"Would you like his number?" she suggested.

Lyndy's already tense muscles bunched tighter and her patience thinned. "No. We need to see Detective Owens. It can't wait," she added, summoning as much urgency as she could muster without losing her mind.

"I'm sorry, but no. This is an active crime scene. Interfering now could cause us to miss something. Maybe a key piece of evidence. Surely you understand and don't want that." Lee's expression went flat and stern. They wouldn't get past her without a fight. Possibly a physical one.

"Owens," Cade called, cupping his hands around his mouth. "Owens!"

Lee unleashed the handcuffs from her belt and muttered something about obstruction. She clamped a hand on his arm.

"No!" Lyndy yelped. "Please! Don't! We'll go. I swear. Please don't take him from me, too." Her mouth clamped shut at the slip of that final word, and Lee released Cade as if she'd been burnt.

Owens strode into the hallway, concern etched deeply on his brow. "Lyndy?" He opened his arms to escort Lyndy and Cade aside. "Is everything okay?"

"No." She choked out the word as tears began to fall.

Gus began to cry with her, shaken by her sobs and the tears dripping onto his cheeks.

Cade turned her toward him. "Give us a minute," he told Owens. "Don't leave."

He pulled Gus free from the sling and cradled him against his broad chest, shushing and bouncing her son until his cries morphed into a babbled tirade of complaints.

Lyndy wiped her eyes and popped a pacifier into Gus's little mouth, then kissed his head. "Thank you," she mouthed to Cade, deeply moved by his ability to save the moment. His continued willingness to go above and beyond for her and Gus.

"What can you tell us about what happened here?" Cade asked, squaring off with the detective while comforting her baby, as if it was the most natural thing in the world.

Owens looked from Cade to Lyndy, then back, curiosity pinching his brow. "You've probably heard the victim was Ramona. Beyond that, we don't know much. There were no signs of a break-in, but there was clearly a struggle to the end."

Lyndy crossed her arms, attempting to hold herself together. "Was it him again?" she asked, already knowing the answer. The Kentucky Tom Cat Killer had been there. Had murdered another woman just a few yards from where she stood. With Gus. Her throat thickened and her breaths came short and fast.

She'd brought her infant to a murder site. What was wrong with her? What kind of mother was she?

"We believe so," Owens said.

Cade scoffed. "You know this was her manager from the smoothie shop. There weren't any signs of forced entry because she knew him. And he knew how to find her from employee records. Ramona knew it was Terri buying Lyndy's smoothies last year. He knew we'd make the connection."

Owens rubbed his forehead, aging before her eyes. "I don't disagree. Problem is, without Ramona, our theory becomes circumstantial at best, and that's a stretch."

Lyndy bristled. "Have you talked to Terri? Did you get Cade's message about the muscle cream? Does Terri own or use that brand?"

"Unfortunately, we haven't been able to reach him," Owens admitted. "I've been here all morning, but my men are out looking. Trust that we're building a case. Collecting facts that, when combined, will hopefully tell the story of who's behind these things, explicitly and without room for reasonable doubt. We will get our man, Ms. Wells."

Lyndy leaned instinctively against Cade's side, exhausted, deflated and in need of his seemingly endless strength.

His arm wrapped instantly around her. "Why can't you reach Terri? What does that even mean?" Cade asked Owens, pulling the words straight from Lyndy's mind.

"It means he's not at home or at the local shop, and he's not answering his phone, but there are lots of reasons people can't be reached. You couldn't reach me two hours ago."

"We're here now," Cade said. "And it's a small town. How long have your men been trying to reach Terri?"

Owens lifted his palms, indicating Cade should settle down. Lyndy bit the insides of her cheeks to keep from screaming.

"You need to be patient while we try to make

sense of what's happening here, but we will. That's a promise."

A dark, humorless laugh erupted from Lyndy's core. "Sense?" she snapped. "How will any part of his murderous rampage ever make sense?"

"What about Terri's friends or neighbors?" Cade asked. "Surely someone has a guess about where he could be."

"They assume he's at work," Owens said. "Terri manages four Sunshine Smoothies in Kentucky."

"Where?" Cade asked, his tone low and threatening.

Owens released a long, slow breath. "One in each of the counties where a connected fatality has occurred."

Lyndy's head lightened and her stomach jolted. "So you know it's him. You aren't looking for him so you can question him. You're trying to find him so you can arrest him. And you can't." A sheen of panic-induced sweat broke over her forehead as the terrifying reality of that settled in. "What's left to keep him in check now? If he knows he's going to be arrested? If he's backed into a corner?" She recalled the way Terri had cornered her in the hallway outside the ladies' room, offering her free smoothies and wondering how she was holding up. All while knowing he was the one responsible for her misery. While he plotted his next grab at her.

She clenched her jaw as her teeth began to chatter. "Did Sanchez tell you the flowers sent to my office with Ramona's badge were identical to the ones sent to Carmen's hospital room?" Lyndy asked. "I'm worried that could be significant."

Owens grimaced, his gaze flicking from Lyndy to Cade, then back. "Carmen was released from the hospital this morning, but we haven't been able to reach her."

Chapter Fifteen

Cade piloted his truck across county lines with a white-knuckled grip. He'd never been so eager to put distance between himself and any specific place since his return stateside. Every instinct in his body told him to keep driving. Pass Fortress Defense, leave Kentucky, leave the Midwest, leave every trace of Lyndy's former existence in their dust and hole up in a cabin off the grid somewhere. Maybe then he could keep her safe until the Kentucky Tom Cat was caught. Until then, there was no room for error, and Cade was making far too many mistakes.

Unfortunately, stealing her and Gus away to a cabin off the grid would probably sound a lot like kidnapping to Lyndy, and she had enough reasons to be wary already. He rolled his shoulders and let his head rock left then right, trying and failing to ease the painful tension gathered there.

Beside him, Lyndy slept. She'd gone silent just outside her town, then began breathing deeply as they'd made their way onto the turnpike. Gus had outlasted her for a bit, whacking at the plastic reindeer attached to his car seat and cooing out a song that only he knew. Then, slowly, the song had faded and his little snores had fallen in sync with his mother's.

Cade had turned down the radio to better hear the sweet sound.

He exited the turnpike an hour later and took the long route through his town, keeping careful watch on his rearview as he had from the start. The truck cab went dark as he eased them into the underground parking area reserved for Fortress Defense team members and guests.

Lyndy stirred as they circled the space. "Cade?"

"Yeah." He squeezed her hand on the seat between them. "We're here."

She straightened with a jolt, tired eyes on alert. "I fell asleep." She twisted for a peek at Gus, then turned back to the cavernous parking area ahead. It was about ten times the number of spots Fortress Defense needed, but it came with the building, which had been exactly what they'd needed. From the metal interior-locking doorways to the extensive camera and security system already in place, the foreclosed property had felt like a sign to him and his teammates. This was what they were meant to do.

Cade cut the engine and went around to help Lyndy out. "Welcome to Fortress," he said, hoisting Gus in his car seat and leading Lyndy to the building's foyer.

Her gaze drifted over the tile floors and freshly

painted walls, then the elevator doors marked with a large Fortress Defense logo. "Wow."

His chest puffed with pride at the little word. Cade had put everything he had into this business. Heart, soul and savings. And her approval meant more than he'd expected. "Wyatt and Sawyer are meeting us inside."

"Your teammates?"

"Yeah. Starting Fortress was Wyatt's idea. He was the first of us to be discharged. He brought Sawyer on next. Then Jack and me."

"How'd you meet Sawyer?" Lyndy asked, following him onto the elevator.

He cast a sidelong look in her direction. "Sawyer's my brother."

The doors closed, and Lyndy's eyebrows rose, then a smile bloomed. "The picky eater?"

Cade warmed impossibly further to the woman beside him. She'd somehow remembered his story about making meals from scraps.

The doors parted before he could answer and a small group of faces stared back at them. Sawyer, Wyatt and their significant others.

Cade groaned at the sight of the crowd. Lyndy had had a bad enough day without having to be personable and make small talk with two extra strangers. Not that the guys would bother her. Neither of them was any more talkative than Cade, but the women... He sighed inwardly, recalling the first time he'd met each of them. Their questions had seemed endless. Intrusive. Exhausting.

Lyndy touched a self-conscious hand to her bruised face.

Cade pulled her fingers away, locking them with his own. "You don't have to worry about that here," he said quietly. "Not with them." If there was an upside to the bombardment she was about to walk into, at least these women had an idea of what Lyndy was going through. They'd both been through recent ordeals of their own.

The Fortress Defense floor plan was open at the center with offices and halls flowing out like spokes in a wheel. A seating area had been arranged several feet from the elevator. Comfortable chairs, a couch, end tables and a bar with water, snacks and coffee when someone bothered to brew it. Thankfully, someone had.

Sawyer opened his arms as he headed in Cade and Lyndy's direction, then pulled his little brother into a quick but firm embrace. "Any trouble on the trip?"

"None," Cade answered, stepping free. "You didn't tell me you were bringing the whole family."

"I didn't," Sawyer said. "It's just Emma and me. She thought she could help."

"Hi." Emma stepped forward and raised a hand hip-high in greeting. "I'm Emma. Sawyer's fiancé."

Sawyer grinned at the introduction, then wrapped an arm around her waist.

"Hi." Lyndy worked up a small smile that didn't reach her eyes. "I'm Lyndy. This is my son, Gus."

Sawyer, Emma, Wyatt and Violet chimed in with coos and welcomes to the baby.

Cade lifted Gus's seat to give him a better look at the crowd. "Lyndy Wells, Gus, this is my brother Sawyer Lance. You just met Emma Hart. And this," he pointed to the couple hanging back, "is Wyatt Stone and his wife Violet."

The group exchanged pleasantries with Lyndy, who looked borderline bewildered.

Cade narrowed his eyes on Sawyer. What had he and Wyatt been thinking, dragging their women in for this? The trip to Fortress was supposed to be for stocking up on surveillance equipment, not social hour.

Violet reached for Lyndy's arm and pulled her toward the couch while Emma descended upon her in a flurry of comforting words and offerings.

And here we go, he thought.

"Oh, honey. It's going to be just fine," Emma said.

"Have a seat," Violet instructed. "Let's get you some coffee and something sweet. Do you like hot chocolate? We brought cookies."

"How old is your baby?" Emma asked, taking Gus's seat from Cade's hand. "Look at those eyes!"

Wyatt tipped his head and moved toward the arsenal and stock room. Sawyer followed.

Cade gave Lyndy another look. She was on the couch now, her feet up and a hot cocoa in hand. Violet had Gus in her arms, and Emma was doling out tissues to blot Lyndy's tears.

He hurried after his teammates, a strange new emotion constricting his chest. Was it gratitude? To Emma and Violet for making Lyndy comfortable? To his teammates for having the forethought to bring their significant others? For the Universe for aligning these things? He entered the next room to find his brother staring.

Wyatt hefted a full pair of duffel bags from the shelf and passed them to Cade. "I packed everything you requested, using your texts as a checklist. Jack's meeting you at Lyndy's place tonight. He's got some time between gigs and gets restless."

"Right." Cade should've guessed it would be Jack to join them.

Jack Hale was the fourth partner, and like Wyatt, a close friend of Sawyer's. The three of them had become like brothers while serving as army rangers. One more thing Cade envied. Most of the folks Cade had gotten close to overseas had either opted to stay through until retirement or they'd come home early by way of a funeral. Regardless, even in the company of three former military men, Cade was the odd man out. As if Sawyer and Wyatt weren't tight enough before, they'd both recently found love and started families. The change had added a new type of camaraderie to their friendship that Cade didn't begin to understand.

Though he was beginning to envy that, too.

Cade rifled through the duffel bags, quickly assessing the contents, knowing Wyatt never did anything less than two hundred percent. "Thanks."

"So?" Sawyer widened his stance and crossed his arms. "What's up?"

Cade frowned. "What?"

"You always hold your clients' hands?"

Cade cringed internally. He'd gotten so comfortable with Lyndy he'd forgotten to drop the boyfriend facade before introducing her to the crew. Faced with the opportunity to explain himself, he didn't want to. Maybe because he shouldn't have to, but more likely because he wanted the lie to be true. It was getting harder to deny his feelings toward the beautiful, fierce and funny, nurturing and selfless woman. What had started as physical attraction had gotten out of control, and now his heart was involved.

Sawyer's eyes narrowed when Cade didn't respond. He shook his head slowly. "Told you," he said, shooting a look in his best friend's direction. "I knew something was up. Didn't I say so? I knew it on the phone the first time he called."

Wyatt grinned.

Cade shouldered the bags, unwilling to bite. "I've got to get moving if I'm going to set a surveillance perimeter outside Lyndy's place before dark. It's another hour back."

"Give me just a second," Sawyer said rubbing a hand over his stubble-covered cheek. "What was it you told me when I fell for Emma while trying to save her sister?"

Wyatt smiled. "I know this one. I think I heard something similar when I fell for Violet."

Cade turned for the door.

Someone snapped his fingers behind him. "We were asking for trouble," Sawyer said. "That was it."

"No, it was work and romance don't mix," Wyatt said, "especially in this line of work."

"That's right. That, too," Sawyer said.

Cade marched into the next room to grab an extra charger for his phone and more batteries for the cameras.

"We were crossing lines," Sawyer continued, repeating Cade's warnings for him when he'd gone goofy-eyed for Emma while he should've been working. "We could've ruined the company's reputation." He moved into view, ticking off fingers as Cade searched for more AAA batteries.

Cade straightened. "Fine. I shouldn't have said all those things to you. And you could be right about me and Lyndy, but I don't know. For the record, we hold hands because it keeps her in arm's reach and it pisses off her stalker."

His teammates exchanged another look.

"Stop," he warned, zipping the bag over its additional contents. "What was my tell, anyway?"

Sawyer laughed. "I knew the minute you stopped calling her the asset, the client, or Ms. Wells." He made ridiculous air quotes around each of the things

Cade had originally called Lyndy. "You switched to using her first name within twenty-four hours."

"Then, you started saying *we*," Wyatt added. "Day one, you were assessing the client's property. The next morning, you were accompanying Lyndy into town for something or other, and twenty-four hours later, everything was *we*. *We* just had dinner. *We* plan to visit her gym tomorrow. That's how it happens. It starts out about you, then it's all about her, and then you become a *we*."

Cade turned on his heels. That was exactly how it'd happened. "Thank you for the help prepping my supplies, and for your profoundly unwarranted assessment of my personal business."

The men followed on his heels.

Cade slowed at the sound of a familiar newscaster. The women had quieted and turned to face a television mounted on the far wall. They'd also made their way through a sizable pile of cutout cookies.

He dropped the bags near the elevator doors, then headed for his part-time bunk. "I'm going to grab a few of my personal things, and we can head out."

Lyndy nodded without taking her eyes off the screen.

Cade moved down the hall where each of the men kept a bed for late nights, an array of personal items and a few changes of clothes for times they were too tired to make the trip home between jobs. Cade needed everything he had in there and possibly a few things from his place if the assignment went on too long.

Someone pumped up the television volume and the words *Kentucky Tom Cat Killer* drifted down the hall, tightening Cade's muscles. He swiped a backpack off the closet floor and stuffed it with his things while straining to hear the reporter.

"They're interviewing a woman outside a home near here," Sawyer called.

Cade moved a little faster, eager to hear what the woman might say. "Is she a witness? Or a victim?" he hollered.

"She looks a little shell-shocked," Violet said, her voice carrying down the hall as Cade hurried back to the group.

Cade took up position on the couch at Lyndy's side and tuned in to the voice-over, regaling the world with details of the hunt for a serial killer.

Violet was right. The woman in the background seemed harried. She was willowy and had raven hair and dark eyes. And she was visibly pregnant. She gaped at the reporter and camera, then scooped a young boy off the ground and headed for the house behind her. The home was small but charming and well maintained, on a street of similar properties. "Who is she?" he asked again.

Lyndy tilted her poor battered face to look into his eyes. Her small hand slid into his. "That's Terri's wife."

Wife? Cade tried and failed to process the word. Terri, the potential serial abductor, rapist and murderer, apparently lived in a little yellow cottage with flower boxes and a tic-tac-toe board drawn in chalk on his sidewalk. He had a wife, a son and a baby on the way. Was that even possible?

Did this woman live in a secret hell? Or did Terri have two completely different lives, two masks and two personalities?

Or were they all wrong about Terri?

What if the killer was someone else entirely, and everyone was wasting precious time chasing an innocent man while a killer was still on the hunt for Lyndy?

Chapter Sixteen

Lyndy buckled into Cade's truck feeling oddly refreshed. Despite everything else, and the shocking revelation that Terri had a wife, it had been wonderful to sit and talk with the other women at Fortress Defense. Lyndy had walked into the building feeling alone and walked out feeling like part of a team. Others had been in her shoes, and they'd survived. They'd thrived. As thankful as she was for Cade's presence and protection, she doubted he'd ever felt as vulnerable and helpless as she did, and she knew he'd never experienced a mother's fear for her child. But Emma and Violet had. They, too, had been hunted and afraid, all while protecting their babies. And the fact they'd both come out happy gave Lyndy hope. Something she desperately needed.

Cade checked his rearview mirror for the millionth time, probably looking for a killer on their tail. It was hard to tell, and he hadn't said much since they'd arrived at Fortress. He'd traded some pointed looks with his brother before leaving, but none of the men had said much and the tension between them had been palpable.

Lyndy had a feeling the tension was directly related to her, but she wasn't sure how to ask.

He slowed at a traffic light, then made a right into a residential area.

"It was nice that your brother and Wyatt brought Violet and Emma," she said, hoping to break the silence and perhaps find out what had happened between the men that she hadn't seen. "They were really nice. I didn't realize how much I needed that."

His eyebrows rose in response. "I'm nice."

"Yes." She laughed. "You are. I meant it was nice to have girlfriends again for a little while. I lost touch with people after Sam died. It turns out that most of the people I knew in town were through him. Wives and girlfriends of Sam's friends. Without him, they just stopped coming around. By the time I was on my feet again after the funeral, they'd vanished completely. The women at my office are a lot older than me. Their kids are grown. Their lives are different. Spending that time with Violet and Emma made me think I could probably use some mom friends."

"Everyone needs friends," Cade said. "People you trust implicitly. Who have your back. All the time."

Lyndy pursed her lips. She'd had people. Important ones. Her mom. Her grandmama. Sam. They'd all died. And the devastation following each loss hadn't gotten easier. In fact, it was probably good that Cade had shut down her budding feelings for him because she'd have to be crazy to set herself up for another heartache of that magnitude. She turned to watch the town go by, no longer in the mood to talk.

Cade took the next left and huffed out a sigh. "I forgot about the road construction over here. This used to be my shortcut back to my place."

The passing shops and homes seemed strangely familiar, though Lyndy had never been there before. "Where are we?"

"We just entered Bolton." Cade glanced in her direction. "I need a few things from my place. I was going to put it off, but we're already this close. Do you mind?"

"Of course not," she said, oddly eager for a look at the place Cade called home.

"Great. Are we still decorating that tree tonight?" he asked with a wink.

"Sure." She sank against the seatback at the mention of decorating. Cade was trying to make the best of her awful day, but it didn't feel like Christmas to her. Not when another woman had died today and a second was missing. She trailed her fingertip across the cool glass, watching snowflakes land and melt as they rolled through a cute little town.

A cobblestone shop caught her eye and she straightened. "I know that café." She'd seen it on the news.

The truck slowed, and Cade gave the world around them a more thorough exam. "Did the newscaster say Bolton?"

"He said Jefferson County when the clip started." She peered down each street as the truck regained speed. "What if he's here? What if he's in the crowd around his house? Enjoying the chaos."

"The cops know what he looks like. They'll spot him."

Lyndy chewed her lip as a throng of walkers came into view, all moving in the same direction. The streets were crowded up ahead, narrowed by parked cars on either side, and the number of pedestrians continued to thicken.

Cade didn't respond as he fell into the line of traffic attempting to get through the congestion.

Lyndy sat taller, suddenly feeling like a live wire, nearly certain this was the block of homes she'd seen on the news. Her attacker lived here. Carmen's attacker. Ramona's killer.

Watching that poor woman learn that her husband was being sought by the police as the main suspect in a serial killer investigation was gut wrenching. And the woman was pregnant. Visibly so, maybe near the end of her last trimester. And there was another small child with her. A boy, like Gus.

The scene had been surreal. She'd imagined Terri living alone in an apartment over his parents' garage or at a run-down hotel in the boondocks. She'd assumed he spent his free time creating and maintaining a creepy stalker wall complete with surveillance photos and planning his next abduction. Not in suburbia with a pretty young wife, child and a baby on the way.

How could he be both a normal, productive member of society and a monster?

A news van barreled past them at the next intersection, and Cade cursed.

He adjusted his grip on the wheel, then pressed on, following the van down the narrowed road. Police cruisers blocked the road ahead. An officer leaned close to a car window, pointing in their direction while another redirected traffic.

Clusters of people lingered on the corners and along the sidewalks, watching the pretty yellow cottage across the historic brick street. Neighbors loitered under pretense of collecting mail from snow-covered boxes, shoveling their drives or clearing their windshields, but were blatantly fixed on Terri's home where a police cruiser and news van shared the drive.

"It all looks so normal," Lyndy said. "Aside from the mass interest."

Cade grunted, his jaw tight. He pulled into the nearest driveway and performed a three-point turn, heading back the way they'd come and cutting down an unobstructed alley between picket-fenced backyards. "He's one of those guys who all the neighbors will say was polite and kept to himself. The guy no one suspected."

The driver's-side door opened on a parked sedan at the back of the yellow cottage, and a familiar detective climbed out.

"Look!" Lyndy pointed, her finger bobbing and heart hammering. "It's Owens! If he's here, it could mean they've got Terri in custody. Pull over." She tugged her mittens over shaky hands and hopped out the moment Cade shifted into Park.

"Detective Owens!" she called as he meandered up the red cobblestone walk. Her voice was lost in the clamorous shouts and horn honks stretching from the chaos out front.

Owens scanned the snowy yard as he moved, stopping to tug the door on a small yellow shed.

"Detective Owens!" she tried again, sliding as her feet slid on frozen stones outside the truck.

He turned on the steps, tracking the sound with his gaze, and his expression turned to shock at the sight of her. "Ms. Wells?"

Lyndy exhaled a long sigh of relief. She unfastened Gus's seat as Cade rounded the bumper and met her on the walkway.

"I've got Gus," he said, taking the car seat in one hand. He reached for Lyndy with the other.

Lyndy gripped his hand tightly as they hurried in the detective's direction. "Did you find him?" she asked, breathless with hope.

Muffled sobs and the distant sounds of an unhappy child drifted from the little home behind him. Agent Maxwell opened the door. "Detective?"

Owens raised a palm to hold off the man. Lyndy stared, immediately reminded of the morning Owens and Maxwell had come to her house to deliver the horrific news that the man who'd attempted to nab her the night before was believed to be a serial killer.

"Who's there?" The pregnant woman from the news arrived in the open doorway at the man's side. Her eyes were red with tears, her face puffy from crying. Her gaze leaped to Lyndy's bruised and stitched face. "Oh dear." Her knees buckled, and Maxwell released the door in favor of catching the woman.

A preschool-aged boy screamed at the sight of the collapsing woman.

The sounds of heavy footfalls and a dozen voices registered in the alley behind them.

Owens waved a hand to Lyndy and Cade. "I suppose you'd better come in."

Owens shut the door behind them, and the woman stared at them through glossy eyes. The agent had sat her in a chair, the child had climbed onto her small lap. She wrapped her arms more tightly around him as her bottom lip quivered. "Did Terri do this to you?" she asked. "Did my husband hurt you?"

Lyndy touched her battered face on instinct.

The agent braced his hands on his hips. "Why are you here?"

"We were leaving Fortress Defense and got stuck in the chaos," Lyndy answered, the words rolling effortlessly off her tongue as she stared back at the petite woman before her. "I saw Detective Owens and thought it meant he'd made an arrest. Maybe he was here to let Mrs. Fray know." She pressed her lips tight to stop from saying more.

Mrs. Fray's gaze slid to Gus, snoozing comfortably beneath a quilted blanket, his small face framed by the earflaps of his favorite winter hat. "I'm so sorry," she whispered, then burst into heart-wrenching, frame-shaking sobs.

The little boy on her hip slid to the floor and clung to her leg, also crying now.

"She's been like this since we got here," the agent said, addressing Detective Owens. "We're waiting for permission to search the house or a warrant, whichever arrives first, and we still need to interview her."

Lyndy moved into the room, snagging a box of tissues from a nearby stand and delivering them to the woman's hands. "Do you want to move someplace more comfortable? Your bed or the sofa? You can put your feet up," she suggested softly.

The woman lifted her face, remorse and gratitude blending in her teary eyes. "Sofa."

Lyndy knelt to speak with the boy. "Hi." She wiped the tears from his cheeks. "Can you help me? I want to take your mama to the sofa, but I've never been here before."

He nodded, then stood. And like a little angel who loved his mama, he led the way through their kitchen and into a sweetly decorated sitting area near the front of the home.

Lyndy wrapped an arm around Mrs. Fray and

helped her follow. She patted the boy's head, then crouched beside his mother. "Can I get you anything? Maybe some water or a cold rag for your neck or eyes?"

The woman choked back a heavy sob. "Why are you helping me?"

Lyndy's broken and mangled heart lodged in her throat. "I was about that pregnant not long ago." She let her gaze fall to the baby bump beneath Mrs. Fray's dress. "I remember how uncomfortable it can be. I know what it's like to be pregnant and devastated."

The woman swung her feet onto the cushion beside her and cradled her arms around her middle. "I can't believe this is happening."

"I know," Lyndy agreed. It was exactly the way she felt, and she couldn't imagine what it would feel like to be Mrs. Fray. "I'm Lyndy."

"Jane."

"Jane." Lyndy smiled. "How about your son?"

Jane worked a tissue under her eyes. "Alex."

Cade and the other men stood silently at the edge of the room.

The home was as charming inside as out. The tree dripping with twinkle lights and handmade ornaments. A handful of wrapped gifts waited on the red-and-white velvet skirt beneath.

The cottage walls were pale blue and trimmed in wide white woodwork. Doilies centered tables and decorative pillows topped seats. Dozens of family photos lined the walls.

Lyndy watched as Jane wiped her eyes, wondering what she could possibly say to comfort a pregnant woman whose husband might be the man trying to kill her.

"Did my husband do that to your face?" Jane asked, her eyes refilling with tears as she awaited the response.

"Maybe," Lyndy said, her throat suddenly parched and tight. "I bet you can help the agents figure that out."

"He rapes women?" she asked, the words little more than squeaks. "He murders them?" Jane covered her mouth, the final words barely audible.

Lyndy willed herself to be strong, even as she shivered with a terror-inducing rush of memories. "You have to help us," she whispered. "If it's not Terri, then you can help clear his name, but if it is, then you can help stop him."

"He's my husband," Jane cried. "My son's father. My baby's." She curled forward, hunching her body protectively over her bump once more. "It can't be true. This can't be real."

"Jane," Lyndy said, "It's very real, and I know you don't want to deal with any of this right now, but if you don't tell us where your husband is, the next time he gets his hands on me, my son will be left without a mother."

Chapter Seventeen

Twenty minutes later, Cade watched, impressed and mildly astounded, as Jane took her seat at the head of the dining room table. She sat poker straight, expression tight and ready to deal with the inexplicable catastrophe her life had suddenly become. The change was extreme and borderline miraculous, but Lyndy had been with her each step of the way. She'd made coffee, found Jane's phone and the sitter's number, then doled out a pair of aspirin.

Soon, the woman had rallied. In the face of near-paralyzing grief and heartache, she'd squared her shoulders, wiped her tears and asked the sitter to take Alex out for cocoas and sledding. Then she'd given Agent Maxwell her blessing to have a team search her home, and she'd gone inside to clean herself up.

Now the five of them sat at the dining room table. Three men with coffee. Two women with iced water. Cade and Lyndy on Jane's left, Detective Owens and Agent Maxwell on her right. Gus lazed in his mother's arms, enjoying a bottle.

"I've seen the news," Jane said softly. "I've heard about the man they're calling the Tom Cat, but I haven't paid much attention to the details. It seemed so completely separate from my life, like a thing that had nothing to do with me and was none of my business. I thought it didn't matter because I didn't fit the profile." She folded her hands on the table and inhaled audibly, releasing the breath through thin, tight lips. "Help me understand who you're looking for and why you think that man is my husband."

Lyndy leaned against Cade's shoulder, the warmth and weight of her steadying him.

He hoped she knew he was there for her. Whatever she needed. And he knew he had to make that clear at his next opportunity.

Across the table Maxwell rattled off an unnecessarily cold and forensic recount of the Kentucky Tom Cat Killer's crimes, dates and locations. Heinous crimes he now accused Jane's husband of committing.

She shuddered in response.

"Stop," Lyndy interrupted, reaching for the woman's trembling hand. "That's enough." She locked a heated gaze on the agent, and Cade squelched a smile. "Maybe Detective Owens can take it from here."

The agent frowned but relented, and the older detective picked up with a profile that fitted Terri to a T.

Cade's heart swelled with nonsensical pride for the woman beside him, who'd officially stolen his heart. He'd never seen kindness given with the wholehearted compassion and conviction that Lyndy showed. And her tenderness was next-level for anyone, but under such duress, it was nearly unfathomable. Wasn't it only an hour ago that Violet and Emma had comforted Lyndy? Now she was here, advocating for the woman whose husband had attacked her twice. Wouldn't any other victim want to scream at Jane for being blind or willfully ignorant? Wouldn't another person in Lyndy's place even blame Jane for the situation. For not seeing her husband as the psychopath he was and turning him in? Cade wouldn't have blamed those women, but he admired Lyndy.

"I see," Jane said, drawing Cade's attention back to the conversation at hand. "It's true that Terri can be a little distant and demanding, but he's not capable of those things. He's too self-contained and tidy." She lifted a hand to indicate the home around them. "Terri is centered. He likes everything in its place, and he's clean to a fault. The trauma of attacking someone, of fighting a woman or hurting her would be too much. It's just not who he is."

"But he is distant and demanding," Maxwell said, repeating her words. "He's clearly hyper-organized. Controlled to a fault, wouldn't you say?" He cast an intentional gaze to the small coatrack visible near the back door. Coats were zipped neatly on hangers, all facing the same direction. Shoes and boots beneath, each lined carefully by the heels, according to style, then color, dark to light. "The pathological need to control is often associated with men who do outrageous things."

Jane sipped her water, then pressed her palms to the table and averted her eyes. "Terri has no reason to rape. He comes home frequently to me, and I'm always available." Her cheeks reddened at the disclosure. "Anyway, he's often too tired when I make the suggestion. His job takes a lot out of him."

The men across from Cade exchanged a look.

"Mrs. Fray," Detective Owens said carefully. "The calm you see could be a recuperation period of sorts, a downtime, after high intensity acts of violence elsewhere. And for the record, rape is never about sex. It's always about dominance and control."

Jane sat back in her seat, gaze distant.

Maxwell retrieved a small notebook from his jacket pocket and made a notation, then cleared his throat. "How did your husband injure his arm, Mrs. Fray?"

"Racquetball." She answered, surprise arching her brow. "How do you know about that?"

Cade frowned, no longer able to butt out. "He wears a sling that's hard to miss. When we asked him about it, he said the injury happened six weeks ago. Is that true?"

"I suppose, but I haven't seen him wear the sling in a month. He said it was too cumbersome and the doctor gave him an all clear almost right away. When did you speak to him?"

"This week," Cade said. "His doctor gave him a nearly immediate all clear on a torn rotator cuff?"

She wrinkled her red nose. "A what?"

One of Maxwell's men emerged from the nearby hallway with evidence bags and a concerned expression. He arranged the bags inside a cardboard Bankers Box on the kitchen island, then stared at Maxwell.

"Excuse me," Maxwell said, stretching onto his feet and crossing the small space into the open kitchen. "What do you have?" he asked, voice low.

Detective Owens went to join them while Cade, Lyndy and Jane listened in.

"Several small weapons," the other agent explained, using gloved hands to handle the bags and materials inside. "A number of palm-sized blades and two slings fitted with makeshift interior pockets, presumably to store and hide the blades. I've flagged a number of websites and transactions on the family laptop." He paused to glance in Jane's direction, his expression going grim. "And a false floorboard in the home office, covering what appears to be a stash of mementos."

Jane pushed onto her feet and swayed from the effort. "What does that mean? Mementos?"

Lyndy moved Gus against her chest, setting his finished bottle aside and reaching for Jane's hand. "You should sit."

"Then we're right?" Cade asked. "It's been Terri all along?"

The agent with the bags gave a tiny nod.

Maxell lifted a palm. "We'll need to send these items to the lab before we know what we have."

Cade scoffed. He checked his watch, then turned to Jane. It was well after five, and he still had to drive back to Lyndy's, meet Jack and set a surveillance perimeter. "Where is your husband now?"

"I don't know," she said, letting Lyndy help her back into her seat. "I told Agent Maxwell. Terri called this morning to say he had to take care of something. The task was unplanned. Unexpected. He apologized and said it would take two days. Alex was screaming about his breakfast, and I didn't ask anything more. I assumed it was another business trip and we'd talk later." She slid her eyes back to the agent who'd been holding the bags. "What kind of mementos?"

Lyndy gripped Cade's fingers on the table between them.

He turned his hand to lace their fingers and gave them a strong squeeze "Where's Terri staying? How can we reach him?"

"Maybe the mementos are my things," Jane said weakly, her voice shaking as badly as her hands. "Maybe he's held on to souvenirs from our past."

"And he hid them under the floor?" Maxwell asked.

Lyndy shot the agent another hard look. "Jane, please," she pleaded. "We need to know where Terri is. Another woman went missing this morning. She barely survived the last time he got ahold of her. I doubt she'll be so lucky again. If these men are right about Terri, and you know where he is, you can help save her life."

"If my husband is a serial killer," she said, her words broken by a swallowed sob.

"If he is," Lyndy said quietly, "where would he take her?"

"I don't know," Jane blurted, hard and loud, startling Gus. "I don't know him. I don't know anything anymore." She covered her mouth and paled. "What does this mean for my kids? Will they be like him? Are they broken?" Tears dripped from her cheeks onto her enormous belly as her body rocked with sobs.

Lyndy pressed onto her feet, looking more exhausted than Cade had ever seen her. "Someone needs to call her doctor," she said. "Jane should be monitored and probably given something to keep her calm. None of this is good for the baby."

Detective Owens returned to the table, reaching for Jane and helping her up. "Do you have someone who can stay with you through this?" he asked.

"My mother," she cried. "I want to talk to my mother."

Cade steadied Lyndy as she swayed. Everything about her expression said she would give anything to speak to her mother right now, too. "Come on," he whispered. "I think it's time we go."

They donned their coats and bundled Gus for the ride home, then moved into the inky darkness amid the falling snow. Cade's heart was full and tight. Full of love, he realized, for the woman and child in his protection. Tight because Terri Fray had told his wife he'd be gone for two days.

Which meant Carmen Dietz had less than forty-eight hours left to live.

Chapter Eighteen

It was after midnight when Gus finally went to sleep. Lyndy nearly wept in relief. This day, like too many before it, had simply been too much for her little guy, and Lyndy completely understood. She'd cheerfully turn in for a week when it was over, if she could, but she suspected she wouldn't rest at all tonight. And she doubted Gus would make it through to dawn without waking. The negative energy and tension in the air was palpable, and everyone felt it, including her little guy.

She crept carefully from the room, tugging the door nearly closed behind her, the speaker of his baby monitor in one hand. When he needed her again, she would know and be there in a heartbeat to comfort him.

Snow fell in continuous white clumps outside the warm farmhouse, piling on windowsills and adhering to the frames. Lyndy paused to admire the way the world shined beyond her small hallway window, a landscape of snow, drifting and glittering as far as the new security lighting allowed her to see. Cade had been working on the lights for hours. His partner Jack had been at her place when they'd arrived, already outlining the work to be done. News of a coming snowstorm had cut the niceties and chitchat short and put the men to work.

So much for decorating the Christmas tree. This year they'd be battening down the hatches against a murderous psychopath on a rampage, instead.

She padded down the hallway in her fleece pajamas and fuzzy socks, ready for bed and knowing the men in charge of her protection wouldn't sleep tonight so that she could. She'd ordered pizza hours ago and eavesdropped shamelessly while Cade brought Jack up to speed on the details of her case. When they'd gone out to walk the property, she'd stayed in the front room near the window and played with Gus, her phone close at hand. Every sound in the quiet home had seemed amplified as she kept one eye on the police cruiser stationed out front and the other on her kicking baby. Thankfully, the men had returned inside an hour with a detailed plan for securing her home and a manageable perimeter around it.

Jack's sharp hazel eyes snapped up to meet hers before she reached the kitchen, an uncanny habit of his. He was seated at her small table, his laptop open before him and a swirl of steam rising from the mug near his hand. The tang of reheated pizza mixed with fresh black coffee in the air. "Everything okay?"

"Yep. You?" She poured a jar of sweet tea and

leaned against the counter, examining the lean man before her. He'd arrived in a Jeep at least as old as himself, which she guessed to be midtwenties. He was unconventionally handsome, with a sandy mustache and beard, but a completely bald head. He listened more than he spoke, and from what she could tell, he didn't miss much. Which was good for her, and hopefully bad for Terri.

"Good."

She sipped the tea and contemplated her next words. She wanted to pull up a chair and ask to be caught up on whatever she'd missed while wrestling with a nearly inconsolable infant for the last two hours, but she didn't know Jack. Cade trusted him, and she trusted Cade, but in many ways, Jack was as new and uncomfortable to her as all the other things that had sprung into her life this week. Her feelings toward him were typical and expected, she presumed. Unlike her feelings for Cade, which had been confusing and powerful from moment one.

Cade had never felt strange or new. Cade felt like coming home.

"Hey." Cade appeared in the doorway, and she smiled. A strange and conflicted expression battled across his brow.

Jack looked from his partner to Lyndy, then excused himself to check on their equipment, leaving her alone with Cade in the kitchen.

"Hey," she repeated, feeling the flight of butterflies in her chest. "Everything okay?"

"No," he said. "Not really." He crossed the kitchen to her in slow, confident strides, then reached for her hands. "We need to finish the talk we were having about why you kept trying to kiss me."

Her cheeks flared and her stomach clenched. "We really don't." He'd made his stance abundantly clear. Cade was there to protect her. Nothing more. "I get it," she said. "And it's okay."

"It's not," he said. His Adam's apple bobbed and his expression darkened as his soulful blue eyes searched hers. "I love you," he said softly, giving her hands a gentle squeeze. "I didn't tell you sooner because I was worried about being unprofessional. Then I realized I was putting my reputation and the reputation of my business first. And I hurt you doing it. I was wrong to do that. I don't ever want to be the reason you're sad, and I won't put anything before you again." Sincerity dripped from the words, evident in his eyes and touch. "Lyndy, I'm truly sorry."

"You love me?" she asked, not quite sure it could be true.

"I do."

Joy burst through her in an explosion of heart-lifting fireworks and she moved onto her toes in response. "I love you, too," she said, locking her hands behind his head and drawing their bodies delightfully close.

Cade gripped her waist and lowered his mouth to hers in the sweetest kiss she'd ever known. He was warm and strong against her. His lips teasing and light. The chemistry coursing between them was electric as his mouth moved with hers. Lyndy tilted her head and parted her lips, eagerly inviting him in, and Cade slid his tongue against hers, hungrily accepting the offer. He wrapped her in his arms as he deepened the kiss and she held on more tightly to enjoy the delicious ride.

He pulled away a few moments later and caressed her cheek as he pressed his forehead to hers. "I have to set the cameras up before the storm takes over, but I think we should continue this conversation when I come back inside."

She bit her happily swollen lips and smiled. "Me, too."

Cade dressed in his coat and hat, then slipped through her French doors into the cold.

Jack returned to her table without a word.

The night seemed warmer and more full of hope than it had before, as Lyndy busied herself tidying the kitchen. She replayed the kiss on a loop in her head, eager to see the camera work finished and her hero return. Cade Lance loved her, too! She could hardly believe her good fortune in a week of pure misery, but she was immeasurably glad.

She ripped the crust off a slice of pizza before putting the box in her fridge. She'd barely finished a single slice when the delivery was still warm, and she'd been longing to get back to it. Gus had been too tired and miserable to be comforted by Cade, who'd tried to bounce and cheer him so Lyndy could eat, but sometimes, Lyndy knew, there was no substitute for Mom.

She finished the crust, then put the rest of the slice on a napkin and made her way to the table with it and her jar of tea. "How's it going?" she asked Jack, peering over his shoulder at the laptop before him. The screen was divided into numerous, somewhat alien-looking images. All grainy, and strangely lit, presumably from the cameras' night-vision modes. The scenes changed as Jack tapped a fingertip against his wireless mouse, showing a variety of points and angles around her home's exterior.

"Wow. You have been busy." She strained for a glimpse of Cade, but he was nowhere to be found. Just the darkest of nights, streaked with the endless contrast of seemingly luminous white snow. Wind beat through the little laptop speakers, sending shivers along Lyndy's spine. "Notice anything unusual out there?" she asked, nearly holding her breath for the answer.

"No." Jack clicked the mouse faster, forcing the images into a streaky black-and-white blur until Cade came suddenly into view. He crouched near the small outbuilding where she'd once dreamed of cooping chickens in the backyard.

Her lungs expanded at the sight of him, strong and steady in her sight. He bent and stretched, working with the cables and camera despite the dropping temperatures and blustering winds. Doing all he could to protect her and her son.

She'd truly enjoyed spending time with him at his office, meeting his teammates and their significant others. The too-short experience had sparked a need in Lyndy she hadn't realized she had. And she longed for the things she'd almost forgotten. Like the joy of community and the importance of a strong social network. Of family and friends who were there for one another. Cade had a fantastic collection of people who loved him, and she hadn't had that in a very long time. She promised herself to begin building something like it for herself once Terri was caught and she and Gus were safe again. She could only hope that Cade would consider staying on to be part of it.

"You're going to be okay," Jack said, his eyes meeting hers in the reflection of his laptop screen. "We're good at what we do, and Cade's a force of nature when he's protecting something that matters. I don't know what went down between you two while I was on my last assignment, but you clearly matter to him. I'll almost feel bad for this Tom Cat if Cade gets ahold of him. He'll have that guy begging to be arrested."

Lyndy laughed at the ridiculous and unexpected imagery. "Let's hope you're right."

And like a glutton for heartache, she let herself imagine what it would be like if Jack was right. What if Cade truly cared for her the way she cared for him? What if one day she was like the ladies she'd met at Fortress? Sitting with Emma and Violet, comforting another woman facing unfathomable danger. Lyndy could be someone else's proof that things would all work out. Being a part of that and belonging to Cade the way Emma belonged to Sawyer or Violet belonged to Wyatt was a fantasy she'd fall asleep to long after Cade had gone, no doubt.

The winds beat against Jack's laptop speakers and howled around the doors and window frames. "Storm's starting to pick up," Jack said.

Lyndy turned for a look through the patio doors overlooking the rear yard. The storm was doing more than just starting to pick up. "It's a whiteout."

The lights flickered around her, dimming then flashing before blinking completely out. Lyndy clutched the countertop, terror-stricken and breathless.

Jack cursed.

"It's just the storm," she whispered, moving seamlessly into action. A summer storm had left them without lights the month Gus was born, and she'd been unprepared. This time, she wasn't. "I've got battery-powered lanterns and candles." She accessed the flashlight app on her phone a moment after Jack illuminated his, then began to unpack her tackle box of batteries and flameless candles.

"Lance, you there?" Jack asked, cell phone pressed to his ear. The beating sounds of wind through his laptop speakers had gone silent with the lost electricity, and the images on the laptop had gone black. A battery backup kept the screen on, but the cameras needed electricity to do their jobs.

"Yeah." Cade's voice boomed across the phone's speaker, and Lyndy nearly collapsed with relief.

"Power's out at the house," Jack said. "And we lost the cameras."

"Storm's here."

"What do you want to do?" Jack asked. "Press on or go to Plan B? Fortify the doors and windows for tonight? Get the cameras back online in the morning?"

Lyndy shook her hands out hard at the wrists, then got to work illuminating and placing battery-operated lanterns and candles around the room. Cade and Jack couldn't work if they couldn't see, but she could provide light. And as long as the gas furnace stayed on they'd be warm.

When the kitchen and living room flickered with the warm glow of a dozen strategically placed candles and two dozen tea lights, she breathed a little easier.

"Lyndy?" Jack called, zipping his thick black parka to his chin. "Can you watch the laptop for me? I'm meeting Cade at the outbuilding. We might be able to get the cameras up with your generator."

"The generator?" Lyndy had forgotten it existed. Sam had picked it up at an auction shortly after they'd bought the farm, but she hadn't seen it or thought about it in ages. "I'm not sure it works."

"It does," he said. "Cade's already got it running. We've just got to get its power to the cameras."

A smile curled her lips. "Perfect."

"Lock up behind me, then give me or Cade a call when the cameras come on."

Lyndy obeyed, carefully securing the door and watching as Jack moved through the storm and into the night. She took his seat in front of the laptop at her kitchen table and bobbed her knee frantically, waiting for the cameras to come back on. Time ticked by inside in gonging silence. Outside, the wind howled and the windowpanes rattled. Lyndy tried not to panic.

She chewed her lip until it ached, then nearly squealed in relief as the laptop screen began to show signs of life. Her home remained in relative darkness, battery-operated candles aside, but the men had gotten their security perimeter back up as promised, and camera by camera, the images reappeared on-screen.

She swiped her phone to life, prepared to share the good news with her heroes when her phone began to ring instead. An incoming call from Jack's number. "Hey!" she perked. "You did it!"

She clicked the mouse, flipping through the images like she'd seen him do, and something strange caught her eye on-screen. A figure that looked like Jack lay sprawled in the snow, arms and legs splayed at awkward angles.

"Hello, Lyndy," Terri growled, his voice spilling like poison through the line. "I've got one down and one to go," he said.

"No!" she yipped. "No, please. You don't have to do this." She stared hard at the screen, willing

Jack to stand up, begging Cade to find him and save him. Praying Cade would reach Terri before Terri reached her.

"You're right," he agreed too easily. "I don't have to. I don't even want to. You know what I really want."

"Me." Tears blurred her eyes. It had all been leading to this, and Terri had won.

"That's right. Why don't you join me willingly, then I won't have to put bullets in the two lawmen out front or your boyfriend out back? I have to tell you, if you make me do that, there's no promises about how your baby will fare."

Bile rose in Lyndy's throat as she imagined the amount of damage she could cause by staying. Somewhere deep inside, she'd always known it would come to this. Maybe that was why the universe had sent Cade her way. Not so he could love her, but because he would see that Gus was cared for. Somehow, after her death.

The silhouette of an outstretched arm, gun in hand, appeared on the bottom corner screen. Cade worked on the old generator a few yards away.

"Don't," she sobbed, scribbling a note for Gus and for Cade on the back of a logoed pizza napkin. "Don't hurt anyone else. I'm coming."

She donned her coat and mittens, then left the note beneath the silent baby monitor.

Please take care of my baby.

Chapter Nineteen

Lyndy told her future murderer she'd meet him at her bedroom window. With the security lighting down, the east side of her home would be virtually invisible from the street and backyard, masked further by the unforgivable snow. She squared her shoulders, then made her way down the hall, thankful that at least leaving the note meant the last thing she did would protect Gus.

Her mind raced as she crept into her room, struggling between the acceptance of what she knew was to come and the hope that she was wrong. She wanted to live. To see Gus grow up. See his first steps. Hear his first words. She wanted to hear his voice change and cheer when he walked across a stage to accept his high school diploma. She wanted to kiss his skinned knees in childhood and comfort him through his every heartbreak. More than all of that, she wanted him to know how deeply she loved him.

She could only hope Cade would tell him every

day if it came to that, and that just maybe Cade would remember what she'd told him about her bedroom window. She flipped the rusty metal window lock and lifted it with a horrendous squeak. The frame rattled and groaned as she raised it above her head. The pealing shriek that accompanied was like nails on a chalkboard.

But no one came running.

Lyndy gasped as the biting cold rushed over her skin and stole her breath She racked her brain for another idea, some alternative to leaving the safety of her home. She'd hoped the window would be her salvation. She'd counted on it. If not the noise from the window, then Gus's screaming as a result. But the badgering wind had apparently masked the sounds of her window, and Gus had miraculously slept through it.

A silhouette moved into view from the shadows and Terri gave a menacing wave, pistol in hand.

Determined not to put Gus in danger to spare herself, she slung one leg over the sill, then the other. She squeezed the sill with trembling fingers, her heart thundering in anticipation. Of Gus waking. Of feet pounding down the hall to her rescue. Of Cade throwing open her door and saving her one last time. Instead, she was met with endless, deafening silence. Only her ringing ears and the howling wind remained.

Terri latched an impatient hand around her ankle and yanked, jerking her from the sill and landing her against his surprisingly solid chest. His hold was abrasive and painful despite the layers of clothing and coats between them. "Good girl," he whispered.

His hot breath seared a path across her frozen cheeks and temple. "Finally. We can be together." He eased his grip on her, looking her over, taking in every detail from head to toe. "And this time you won't fight," he said. "Understand? At least not until I tell you to."

Her stomach rolled and her cheeks flared with the memory of Detective Owens's words. *Rape is always about dominance and control.*

"Why are you doing this?" she asked. "Why hurt all these women? Why hurt me?"

"I like it," he said simply. "The chase. The fight. The triumph. And I've been waiting a long while for you." He pushed her forward, away from her home, and she gave it one last look.

She closed her eyes against the tears.

Why hadn't Cade noticed that Jack never showed up? Why hadn't he gone looking for him? He should have found her note and alerted the officers. Why was this happening? She stumbled forward, sucking air and trying not to fall over her own feet as Terri shoved. "You didn't hurt anyone else, did you?" she asked, suddenly afraid that Cade hadn't come to her rescue because Terri had made sure he couldn't. "You promised."

"And I promise to deliver my first bullet to your son if you try to run."

She stopped, lungs burning and breath lost. "Did you kill them? The men protecting me?"

He moved to her side for a look into her face, then stroked frozen hair away from her tear-stained cheeks. "Don't worry about them. Right now, you worry about me." He scanned her features, squinting slightly, whether against the wind or something else, she couldn't be sure. "You look just like her, you know. And I hate her. So much."

Lyndy struggled to swallow the boulder of fear in her throat. "Who?"

His fingers grazed her cheek, his expression flat, lost in thought. "My mother. She was a wretched, horrible being who controlled everything. Is that what you'll do with your son, too? Control his every breath?" he snarled. "If not now, then soon. You'll decide where he goes, what he wears, how he spends his time and with whom. Shame him. Isolate him when he doesn't live up to your impossible standards. Hit him, spit on him. Hate him."

Lyndy's jaw locked against the protests piled on her tongue. She'd never do any of those things to Gus, but she was beginning to see why Terri had targeted her and the other women who looked so much like her. His mother was his abuser. The one woman he probably felt he couldn't hurt in return. So he was making up for that now. Punishing all his mother's look-alikes. Lyndy included. Especially her, she realized, the mother of a son.

Without warning, he burrowed his fingers deep

into her windblown locks and knotted them against her skull. "Move."

Terri shoved her forward once more, this time releasing her and causing her to fall. She flailed for balance before landing hard in the snow. Her hands plunged into the icy mix, her knees sinking along with them. "Get up," he seethed, jerking her back to her feet and groping her breast roughly as she came against him with a stumbling thud. He lowered the offending arm to lock her in place, then groaned into her ear.

Bile rose in her throat. "Where are we going?" And why hadn't Cade realized she was missing?

"Barn," he growled, directing their path toward the decrepit old barn where Sam had planned to raise livestock.

Was that where he planned to kill her?

"Where's Carmen?" she asked, suddenly recalling that she wasn't the only woman taken by the psychopath today. Was it too late? Or did the other woman still have a chance?

"She's waiting for us. We're going to play a game."

Lyndy's gut clenched at the onslaught of gruesome possibilities and she lurched forward just in time to lose her meager dinner in the snow. She wiped her mouth as she struggled upright, certain there wouldn't be a miraculous rescue for her tonight. If she was going to survive, it would have to be on her own. She fisted her hands to fight as a second set of footprints registered in the snow.

Cade's prints? Jack's? The officers stationed outside her home?

Hope lifted her heart for one fleeting moment before a small, familiar sound nearly doubled her over once more.

The thin, muffled sound of her infant's cries. Coming from inside the closed barn doors.

CADE STILLED AS a strange noise registered on the raging wind. He turned and waited, listening intently and trying to place the sound. Had Jack been the source? If so, then what was he up to? If not, had Jack heard the brief rumbling, too?

Cade liberated the cell phone from his pocket and dialed his teammate.

A second later, another noise drew his attention in the direction of Lyndy's home. Louder and higher in pitch. The short, shrill blast of unforgiving hinges or perhaps…a window.

Cade's feet were instantly in motion, propelling him through the storm, as he pressed his cell phone to his ear. His gut twisted and sank with an inexplicable understanding. He'd just heard someone force Lyndy's bedroom window open. Somehow her home had been breached while Cade was outside setting up equipment to protect it.

If there was a measure of reassurance in the horrific situation, it was that she wasn't alone. Jack could defend and protect her and Gus until Cade arrived. As long as he realized Terri was there.

The call went to voice mail, and a fresh blade of fear sliced through Cade's chest. He cursed and re-dialed, willing his partner to pick up.

Was Jack fighting the intruder? Was he hiding with Lyndy? Did they know what had happened? Surely Lyndy had recognized the sound.

Cade's sliver of hope turned to panic as a dark figure appeared lying on the ground up ahead.

"Jack!" Cade fell at his friend's side, stowing his weapon and pulling off a glove to check for vitals. "Get up," he snapped, as a strong pulse beat against his fingertips.

Jack groaned and pushed onto his elbows, jerking free of Cade's touch and swaying slightly as he sat. A slew of curses flew from his lips as he rubbed his head, an angry scowl on his previously slack face.

"Come on." Cade clutched Jack's arm and pulled him to his feet. "Terri's inside."

Jack collected his phone and then broke into a run at Cade's side, strides gangly and awkward as his limbs caught up with his will.

Cade pressed his back to the wall outside Lyndy's French doors, anger and adrenaline flowing fast and free through his veins. He turned the doorknob care-fully and eased the barrier open.

Jack crept inside, sidearm drawn, and moved stra-tegically through the kitchen.

Cade headed silently down the hall toward Lyn-dy's room, senses on high alert and stomach rolling with the knowledge of what happened to women who spent time alone with Terri.

A sharp whistle stopped him in place. "Cade!" Jack called, his voice deep and angry, nowhere close to the volume used in pursuit. He strode into view with a scrap of paper in one hand and Lyndy's cordless landline telephone clutched in the other. He pressed the phone to his ear and passed Cade the note with a remorseful frown. "We need boots on the ground," he told whoever he'd called. "Terri's got her. She left a note. Take care of her baby."

Cade's gaze fell to the paper, quickly crushed in his closing fist. He ran for Gus's room, as Jack relayed details of the ugly truth behind him.

He crossed the silent nursery in two determined strides before his heart ripped completely in two.

The crib was empty.

LYNDY'S MUSCLES LOCKED. Her ears tuned to the sound so familiar it could've originated in her heart. "Gus!" She bolted forward, running to the barn and wrenching the door wide. Her baby lay crying, cold and alone in a trough of ancient dirt and hay. His pitiful blanket had been kicked off and his skin was red from the falling temperature. "Gus!" She swept him into her arms and worked the zipper on her coat low, tucking her precious infant inside and cradling his head against her collarbone. "I'm so sorry," she repeated in a whisper, bouncing and shushing him as her already wrecked heart wrenched further.

"A beautiful reunion," Terri said. "I thought it was smart to bring him. In case I need to motivate you once we get where we're going."

Anger boiled in Lyndy's blood as the truth of the setup slowly connected in her mind. "The other set of footprints was yours."

Terri's mouth cocked at one side. "Now we need to get someplace warm. Otherwise your little man could develop frostbite. Start losing fingers and toes. The fingers are looking awfully red already."

Lyndy curled Gus against her more securely, willing her love and body heat to be enough to restore him. She kicked herself mentally as she realized this was her fault. She hadn't checked on Gus before leaving. She'd been too focused on Terri's threats, and his demand she meet him outside.

"Back door," Terri said. "We're almost there now."

"Where?" she whimpered, breathing warm air against her baby's frigid palms.

"To the truck, of course. I borrowed it on my way here, then followed the gravel road that links the dairy farm to your property. It worked out rather well since your second-rate bodyguards made such a small perimeter. No cameras out here. Even if they get that old generator working, we'll be long gone."

"You stole a truck?" she asked, struggling to make sense of anything beyond the fact her infant son had been taken from under her nose and was now being kidnapped along with her.

Terri sneered. "You didn't think I walked here,

did you? In the storm? Surely you've realized by now that I'm a planner. The storm is a convenient assist I hadn't been expecting. Most folks will be inside and off the roads as we leave town. Fewer witnesses."

"Why are you doing this?" she cried. "What about your family? Jane is pregnant and being bombarded by the media and authorities because of you. You're ruining her life and endangering the baby she's carrying. Don't you care? And what about your son? Alex has to grow up knowing what you've done. How can you live with yourself?"

Terri's expression relaxed into the smooth veneer of a man detached. "Those people have nothing to do with this," he said coolly. "They have a nice life because of me. The right house in the right neighborhood. Fancy clothes and the best preschool. Unlike you and your baby, they're going to be just fine."

Lyndy swallowed a sob. The true answer to her question crashed over her head like a hammer. Terri was doing this because he was unhinged, deranged and evil at his core. The real question was how she could survive this time. How could she fight and run while keeping Gus safe inside her coat with no way to secure him there?

"Do you know I watched you every night at the gym?" he asked, controlling the conversation the way he controlled everything else. "I waited for you, hoping you'd come to my shop when you were done, with your ready smile and sweet, freckled face. It was my nightly treat. Just seeing you. Then you stopped coming," he snarled. "And you didn't come back. I took it personally. Then, as fate would have it, I followed Carmen and her friends to the park and saw you there. With him."

Lyndy knew Terri meant Gus. Gus was the only person she'd ever been to the park with. And there was a senseless relief in knowing she hadn't been the reason Terri went after Carmen this week. He'd already had his twisted eye on her.

"Now things are getting back on track. We're finally going to be alone, and I'm going to get to take my time with you. If you don't cooperate, your baby will be sorry." He smiled, and her stomach plummeted.

"Lyndy!" her name echoed in the night outside the barn.

Terri's head jerked in the direction of the calls. "Time to move."

"To where?" she asked, carefully angling her back to him, putting as much space between her son and her assailant as possible. Hoping to drag her feet until she was rescued.

When other voices joined the party outside, Terri jammed the barrel of his gun against her spine and shoved. Forcing her away toward his waiting truck. The barn's big back door swung easily open, revealing a rusted red pickup, nearly covered in snow.

"How long have you been here?" she gasped, wondering if her temporary safety had been a ruse, one more part of his wicked game.

He wrenched the passenger door open with a satisfied smile. "Since your power went out, of course."

Of course. Because he was always one step ahead.

Lyndy stared into the gaping mouth of the stolen truck, its dark interior sure to be the last she and her baby would ever know. She'd read the reports, seen the photos. Whatever happened at their destination would be painful, gruesome and fatal.

She kissed Gus's cold head and felt the devastation of the moment seep into her bones. He rolled his tiny red face up to hers. Eyes wet and wide with tears. His sweet bottom lip jutted forward. His little chest moved in bursts, too short and quick. Breathing air too cold for his infant lungs.

Lyndy's heart expanded with love for her son, and her will grew strong with the knowledge she was his only hope.

She wouldn't get in that truck.

"Lyndy!" Her name was in the air again, louder now. Closer. "Tracks!" Jack called.

She jerked in the direction of the precious sound, and so did Terri.

Her heart lightened the way it had in the alley and resolve curled her arms more tightly around her terrified and whimpering son.

And Lyndy ran.

Chapter Twenty

Lyndy spun in the snow, her body launching into motion. Her legs and heart pumping wildly as she flew through the night.

She couldn't look back. Couldn't stop. Had to believe he wouldn't catch her. Had to trust he wouldn't shoot her as she fled.

Gus flailed, rightly terrified and frustrated as she struggled to keep him safe inside her coat while she ran. His little body shivered and convulsed with panic. His cries ratcheted into Hollywood-worthy screams.

And finally finding her voice, Lyndy joined him.

"Help!" The word exploded from her core in a white puff of fear and desperation. "Cade! Jack!"

Tears blurred her vision as she passed the edge of the barn, pointed in the wrong direction and moving swiftly away from her home, from the road and her protective detail.

"Help!"

Terri's footfalls reached her in seconds, coming swift and sure compared to her awkward ugly flight.

His hand snaked out, catching the hood of her coat, and yanking her off her feet with one sharp pull.

In the next moment, she was airborne, her feet coming up and her body going down. Her back collided with the frozen ground in a teeth-jarring thud. Gus bounced against her chest. The air whooshed from her lungs. She wrapped her arms around him on instinct, cradling his head and body, unable to brace or protect her own. Praying fervently he wasn't injured and that this wasn't their end.

Behind her, the rear barn door slammed open and heavy footfalls pounded the earth.

"Freeze!" Jack called, skidding to a stop several yards away, then moving in slowly. "Officers are on site. And you're done."

Terri cursed as the beams of distant flashlights traced broad paths across the snow in their direction, and the deep, repetitive beating of helicopter blades broke through the blustery night. Searching, she realized, for the Kentucky Tom Cat Killer.

A deep breath of relief flooded her scrambled mind. She and Gus were going to be okay.

Terri put his hands up, then lunged for her, skidding to the ground at her side and gripping the zipper on her coat, attempting to yank it down.

"No!" she screamed and bucked against him, wrestling for control of the fabric, desperate to keep the monster from getting his hands on her baby.

The telltale click of a gun registered like a shot beside him, and he stilled.

Cade stood tall and strong, his outstretched hand only inches from her attacker. "Get your hands off her," he said, the words cold and deadly serious.

Terri released her as a pair of officers appeared behind Jack, guns drawn. The helicopter began to descend, its blinding halo of light illuminating the scene.

Lyndy scrambled backward, pushing her aching and bruised body into a seated position and regaining her hold on Gus. She could no longer feel the freezing wind or falling snow. Couldn't hear beyond the ringing in her ears and the pounding of her heart. She clutched her son instinctively, the effects of shock numbing her mind and senses.

"Terri Fray, you're under arrest!" an officer called, closing the gap between them. "Get down on the ground and put your hands behind your head."

Cade's fierce expression tightened as he lowered his weapon, relenting his position to the lawman. "Do it," he warned, "or this time I will shoot you."

Terri ignored them, staring hotly into her eyes as anguish washed over his face. He'd never touch her the way he wanted. Never hurt her or her son again. Terri had lost the game he'd worked so hard to set up.

In the next heartbeat, he reached into his coat pocket and pulled out his gun.

Her heart seized as a single shot rent the night.

BLOOD SPLATTERED OVER the snow, dousing the immediate area and sending another long scream through Lyndy's lips.

Terri's body jolted forward with the force of Cade's bullet ripping through his flesh, and Cade's lips twisted in grim satisfaction. He would've preferred administering a head shot, but he supposed that wasn't the right thing to do in front of a baby.

He landed a fist against Terri's shocked face, then smashed his boot against the psycho's bloody shoulder, burying it deep into the snow.

Jack kicked the gun away as officers approached. "Told you," he muttered in Lyndy's direction, though Cade couldn't understand why.

He scooped Lyndy into his arms and held her tight, reassuring the three of them that the nightmare was finally over. "Sorry I'm late," he whispered as additional officers and federal agents rushed the scene. He pulled the beanie from his head and stretched it over Gus's hair, then stripped the warm down coat from his body and wrapped it around Lyndy, securing it behind Gus. "Come on," he said. "We need to get you both inside."

"You saved us," she said, emotion flowing through her words and burning hot in her eyes. *Love*, he realized, and recognized it now, because he felt it, too.

"Always," he said, planting kisses on her forehead, then Gus's.

"Paramedics are on the way," an officer called, hauling Terri to his feet and wrenching his arms behind him to administer cuffs.

Cade turned, searching until the promised ambulance trundled into view, plowing slow and steady through the snow, past the old red barn. A pang of intense hope and relief lifted his hand to flag the paramedics down. The killer was caught, but Cade wouldn't find peace until he knew Lyndy and Gus were both going to be okay.

He swept an arm under Lyndy's legs and carried her to safety.

Chapter Twenty-One

Snow drifted magically outside Lyndy's kitchen window, lending a fantastical snow globe quality to her Christmas Eve view. She had a lot to be thankful for this year. The health and safety of her son for starters. Her ability to spend Gus's first Christmas upright and no longer nauseous from the concussion she'd suffered only a few short weeks ago was high on the list, as well. She attributed it all to the unbridled love and devotion of Cade Lance. He had shot the Kentucky Tom Cat Killer after all. Though he wouldn't accept the praise. He preferred to insist it was Lyndy's quick thinking that had gotten him to her in time. They'd reluctantly agreed on a middle ground over sweet tea and snickerdoodles. They were a powerhouse partnership.

No matter how anyone spun it, her life had gone from endangered to enchanted in Cade's arms, and she never wanted anyone else as her partner.

Laughter erupted from the living room where Cade stoked a fire in the hearth and his mother, Mrs.

Lance, danced with Gus in her arms. It was becoming a familiar and beloved scene at Lyndy's house, and she'd surely miss it when the holidays ended. Seeing Cade between jobs wouldn't seem like nearly enough after the way she and Gus had been spoiled these last few weeks.

Cade and his mother had taken turns holding and fussing over Gus around the clock while Lyndy had recovered slowly in bed. Paramedics had immediately diagnosed her little guy with mild frostbite and identified the early stages of hypothermia, both of which were thankfully treatable. Since then, Gus had been swaddled and cuddled enough for ten babies, and the only person more thankful than him was Lyndy.

"Penny for your thoughts?" Cade asked, sliding into place behind her and wrapping his strong arms securely around her middle. He leaned down to press a kiss to her cheek and nuzzle his fantastically grizzly beard against the sensitive skin of her neck. He'd been growing the scruff since they met, and Lyndy was a fan.

She rested her head against his chest and basked in the familiar scent of him. "I'm thinking about how spoiled and happy Gus and I are, partly because Terri was caught. But his family is broken and hurting right now for the same reason. And that makes me a little sad."

Cade's arms tightened around her, the way they always did when Terri's name came up. "Jane and the kids will be okay," he promised. "According to Detective Owens, they've moved back to Jane's hometown and are staying with her parents. She's got a strong support system there to help get her through this." He kissed her head. "And I know you've been worried about Carmen, so I got the scoop from Owens on her, too."

Lyndy craned her neck, immediately filling with hope for the other woman. "You did?"

"Yeah. Carmen's going to be okay," Cade said.

Authorities had located Carmen within hours of Terri's arrest. She'd been terrified, bruised and dehydrated, but otherwise physically okay. Unfortunately, Lyndy had had no idea what had happened to her from there. "How is she?"

"Her mother and sister moved in with her. They're staying until she gets back on her feet."

"That's fantastic," Lyndy croaked, speaking past a growing lump in her throat. "Maybe I'll take Gus to see her tomorrow. I can bring them cookies. Enough for Carmen's mom and sister, too."

"I'm sure they'll like that," Cade said. "There's no such thing as too many friends or cookies."

"True." Lyndy's smile widened. Carmen would love Gus. Everyone did. And she couldn't wait to make the introduction.

"Is there anything I can do to help you in here?" Cade asked.

"I'm just getting paper plates and napkins," she said, feeling slightly guilty that they'd ordered delivery on Christmas Eve, forcing someone else to work so she didn't have to. "Maybe next year I'll make a ham. Gus might even have teeth to try it with by then."

"I love ham," Cade whispered, planting a heated kiss in the hollow beneath her ear. "And have I mentioned I love this dress?"

"You have." She laughed, enjoying the flirtation and feel of his hands on her waist.

It'd been a long time since she'd had enough help with Gus that she could afford the time to get fancied up. She'd forgotten how amazing it felt when she did. Her hair was curled. Makeup and nails were done, and the dress was new, a gift from Cade's mother. She tilted her head for a peek at his face beside hers. "Your mama said she'd keep Gus tonight and bring him back after breakfast tomorrow so I can sleep in. Normally, I'd say he should be here when he wakes, for Santa's sake, but I like the idea of a night alone with you too much to pass up." Besides, at five months old, Gus was more excited about the gift wrap than the gifts.

"Man, I love my mama," Cade said, resting his chin on Lyndy's shoulder. "Bless that woman."

"Indeed." Lyndy blinked against the sting of emotion that always came with Mrs. Lance's kindness. Lyndy missed her own mother so much it hurt, but having Mrs. Lance around these last couple of weeks had been just the emotional therapy she'd needed.

Being a caretaker was nice, but being cared for had been balm to Lyndy's weary soul.

"Any news from the Realtor?" Cade asked, bringing her thoughts back to yet another point of pleasure.

"Not yet," she sighed, "but I suppose it is Christmas." Selling the oversize property she never really wanted and buying something she adored, preferably closer to Cade, was at the top of her holiday wish list.

He pressed a kiss against the curve of her neck and she abandoned the plates and napkins.

She spun in his arms and locked her hands around his back, arching to peer into his sincere blue eyes. "You know we were standing right here the first time you told me you loved me?"

"I love you," he whispered again, drawing her closer and holding her tight.

She slid her palms up his broad chest and drank in his sizzling stare. "And then you kissed me."

Cade's lips were on hers in an instant. A definite perk of having him near. He never seemed to tire of kissing her.

The doorbell rang, and he broke the kiss with a smile. "How do you feel about surprises? And company?"

"I like both, but I'm pretty sure everyone I know is already here, and you've given me more than I need already," she said, suddenly wondering what he was up to. "Plus, we agreed, no gifts."

He wrinkled his nose and raised his shoulders.

"I've got the door!" his mother called. "Gus and I can manage. You two keep kissing. It's Christmas!"

He kissed her nose and grinned.

Lyndy snickered, and Cade took her hand, lifting it to kiss her wrist before leading her toward the living room.

"Wait!" she called. "The plates."

"It's not a food delivery," he said. "Not exactly."

She frowned. "What's that supposed to mean, and how do you know?"

He tapped a finger to his temple as he pulled her along with him to meet the guests spilling into her home.

Jack, Wyatt and Sawyer took turns hugging Mrs. Lance and greeting Gus in his little pajamas printed to look like an elf costume. Each man's hands were heavily laden with shopping bags, all filled with wrapped packages. Emma and Violet each carried a toddler on one hip and a thermal-covered dish satchel in the opposite hand. Behind them Sylvia from the office bounced and waved, her red velvet Santa hat falling over her ears. Detective Owens and his wife brought cookies and fudge, and James saluted Cade from behind a massive poinsettia in his arms.

Tears blurred Lyndy's eyes. "What did you do?" she asked, shocked straight to her toes by the arrival of so many familiar faces in a town where she'd thought of herself as alone. Nurses from the hospital, women from the gym, Gus's day care worker and Officer Sanchez soon followed.

"I thought it would be nice to have some friends over," he said. "I was fielding so many phone calls from folks checking up on you while you were still in bed that I thought I might start asking them to drop by. Every one of them said yes."

Lyndy grinned until it hurt and pulled his lips to hers once more.

Soon, her home was full of warm conversation and laughter. Her heart was filled with unprecedented peace. Detective Owens assured her the Kentucky Tom Cat Killer would never be free again, and she believed him. There was no more room in her world for fear and sadness. Only joy and love and chocolate. She snagged a piece of fudge from Mrs. Owens's pretty tray on the kitchen counter and smiled at the beautiful scene before her. Backlit by her mother's blinking artificial tree and underscored with carols and laughter.

Cade emerged from the crowd a moment later with his mother and Gus on his tail. A throng of guests gathered to follow.

"What's up?" she asked, unable to read Cade's strange expression, a mix of mischief and hope.

He offered her a little velvet box.

She scanned the crowd, his mother's teary eyes and his teammates' knowing looks.

"Cade?" she asked, unwilling to hope for the thing she wanted so badly to be inside the box.

He took her hand in his and lowered to his knee.

A hush rolled through the crowd, but her eyes were fixed on Cade's as he opened the small ring box and revealed the perfect gift.

"Lyndy Wells," he began, his voice low and thick

with emotion, "I have loved you since the day I met you. You make me want to be a better man, and you make me believe I can be. You are smart and loving and fearless, and I don't want to live another day of my life without you by my side. Be my partner in this life. Please, do me the honor of becoming my wife?"

Tears fell hot and fast as her heart overflowed. "Yes," she sobbed. "Yes!"

Cade rose and lifted her in his arms, a look of joy on his suddenly boyish face. "Yes?"

She nodded wildly, and he kissed her deep as the crowd cheered around them.

He set her onto her feet a moment later, too soon as always, and wiped her tears with his fingertips. His smile was brighter than she'd ever seen, and his chest puffed with pride. As if he'd just won a prize of unparalleled magnitude or maybe the Super Bowl all by himself.

"I didn't get you anything," she croaked, waffling between tears and laughter.

"You're wrong about that," Cade said, winding gentle arms around her waist and pressing his forehead to hers. "Baby, you just gave me everything."

* * * * *

Look for the final book in Julie Anne Lindsey's
Fortress Defense miniseries when
Dangerous Knowledge *is available next month!*

And don't miss the previous titles in the series:

Deadly Cover-Up
Missing in the Mountains

You'll find them wherever
Harlequin Intrigue books are sold!

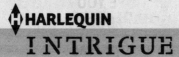

SPECIAL EXCERPT FROM

(H) HARLEQUIN

INTRIGUE

*TCD team member Aria Calletti is determined to find
out why women are turning up dead. The newest victim's
half brother, Grayson Rhodes, has sacrificed everything
to find his half sister and her son. But can a civilian and
a new agent take down a drug kingpin?*

Read on for a sneak preview of
Rookie Instincts by Carol Ericson.

The wind whipped off the lake, its chilly tentacles
snaking into his thin black jacket, which he gathered at
the neck with one raw hand, stiff with the cold. His other
hand dipped into his pocket, his fingers curling around
the handle of the gun.

His eyes darted toward the dark, glassy water and the
rowboat bobbing against the shore before he stepped onto
the road…and behind his prey.

She hobbled ahead of him, her shoes crunching the
gravel, her body tilted to one side as she gripped her
heavy cargo, which swung back and forth, occasionally
banging against her leg.

A baby. Nobody said nothing about a baby.

He took a few steps after her and the sound of his
boots grinding into the gravel seemed to echo through
the still night. He froze.

When her footsteps faltered, he veered back into the
reeds and sand bordering the lake. He couldn't have her
spotting him and running off. What would she do with the

baby? She couldn't run carrying a car seat. He'd hauled one of those things before with his niece inside and it was no picnic, even though Mindy was just a little thing.

He crept on silent feet, covering three or four steps to her one until he was almost parallel with her. Close enough to hear her singing some Christmas lullaby. Close enough to hear that baby gurgle a response.

The chill in the air stung his nose and he wiped the back of his hand across it. He licked his chapped lips.

Nobody said nothing about a baby.

The girl stopped, her pretty voice dying out, the car seat swinging next to her, the toys hooked onto the handle swaying and clacking. She turned on the toes of her low-heeled boots and peered at the road behind her, the whites of her eyes visible in the dark.

But he wasn't on the road no more.

He stepped onto the gravel from the brush that had been concealing him. Her head jerked in his direction. Her mouth formed a surprised O, but her eyes knew.

When he leveled his weapon at her, she didn't even try to run. Her knees dipped as she placed the car seat on the ground next to her feet.

She huffed out a sigh that carried two words. "My baby."

He growled. "I ain't gonna hurt the baby."

Then he shot her through the chest.

Don't miss Rookie Instincts *by Carol Ericson,*
available November 2020 wherever
Harlequin Intrigue books and ebooks are sold.

Harlequin.com

Get 4 FREE REWARDS!

We'll send you 2 FREE Books plus 2 FREE Mystery Gifts.

Harlequin Intrigue books are action-packed stories that will keep you on the edge of your seat. Solve the crime and deliver justice at all costs.

FREE Value Over $20
